Hell Hath
No Fury

BLAKE

Published by Blake Paperbacks Ltd.
98-100 Great North Road, London N2 0NL, England

First published in Great Britain in 1991

ISBN 0-905846-93-1

British Library Cataloguing-in-Publication Data: A catalogue
record for this book is available from the British Library.

Typeset by Maron Graphics, Wembley, Middlesex

Printed by Cox and Wyman, Reading, Berkshire

Cover design by Graeme Andrew
Cover illustration by Paul McCaffrey

1 3 5 7 9 10 8 6 4 2

To Clare . . . .
for putting up with so much.

Acknowledgements

This book started out as a study of killing by women. But it rapidly turned into an intriguing insight into the role played by women in our society.

At first, I presumed that my main sources of information would be the traditional round of policemen and close family. However, *Hell Hath No Fury* eventually became much more than just another true crime book.

Amongst those whose help was invaluable were psychoanalyst Jenny Craddock, who fully explained to me the driving motivation behind so many of these women.

In Australia, Det Sgt Glenn Burton's down-to-earth humour gave me an hitherto unexplored interpretation of the notorious Lesbian Vampire case.

In Brisbane, the crown prosecutor's office of Adrian Gundelach was just as vital.

In North America, Neil Blincow and Drew Mackenzie made an invaluable contribution. It was thanks to their astute observation that I was able to pursue two vital stories in the US. Also many thanks must go to Clare Lissaman, who gave up her valuable time to help my research efforts.

In Germany, TV journalist Tewe Pannier was greatly responsible for the remarkable account of the mother who shot her daughter's killer.

But it was in Britain where so many people rallied to my assistance. The list is too long to repeat here but amongst them were Graeme Gourlay, Susan Barber, Ricky Search, Rupert Maconick, members of the Chantler family and many, many more.

Finally, I particularly want to thank Christine English for her patience and understanding.

Contents

Foreword

"Women have a bloody streak. They don't mind inflicting pain but they don't like making a mess. That is why their favourite weapon is often... poison."

Professor Elisabeth Trube-Becker, who spent twenty-five years studying women murderers.

"A woman who retaliates is deeply threatening to society's view of the family and of man's position in it."

Sociologist Lorraine Radford.

In *Hell Hath No Fury*, I have tried to probe the innermost feelings of the characters involved in each of the awful crimes described here. I want to give you a unique insight into these killings.

During the course of my inquiries, I interviewed policemen, psychiatrists, doctors and social workers, as well as the families of many of the defendants and victims. In some cases, I even managed to talk to the accused themselves.

This is, as far as I know, the first time that such a collection of crimes has been presented in such vivid detail.

I have no doubt that some readers might notice discrepancies between my own accounts of certain cases and what has been reported elsewhere. These differences are always irritating to anyone with a keen interest in the subject, but I have tried to only use information that I believe to be completely accurate. If I have erred in any way at all, I have done so entirely in good faith.

Although these stories read like fiction, everything published is based on fact. Some informed deductions have been made for dramatic purposes (for example the thoughts of people who are now dead) but the actual facts of the case are as they occured.

Wensley Clarkson, 1991

1

The Lesbian Vampire Killers

The sound of cricket-song mingled with the gentle lapping of the river. Every now and again passing cars lit up the roadside as they weaved their way home. The lights from nearby houses went out as their owners retired to bed.

Suddenly, a metallic green saloon span out of the darkness and screeched to a halt in the dusty car-park of the Lew-Mors nightclub. The ten-year-old Holden Commodore had definitely seen better days. An entirely functional car, it was often described as the Vauxhall Viva of Australia. It's shape designed with common sense – and absolutely no style – in mind.

But that didn't worry Bobby. She was a tough, brutal, masculine woman. More concerned with sex, drink and drugs than the remotest thoughts of family responsibilities or any of the standard domestic concerns.

She stumbled into the Lew-Mors with three girlfriends. She was already drunk from having consumed at least ten beers in a tiny bar just half a mile away. As she entered the club, she passed through the tatty lobby and caught a glimpse of herself in a mirror and grimaced. She hated mirrors. They were a sad reflection of her inner self. Then she felt a strange pain in her head. And it wasn't caused by the loud music blaring out from the dancefloor.

This was a pain from within. Bobby was fighting something – but she did not know what.

Once inside the club, Bobby's notoriously promiscuous temperament took over. She had spotted an attractive woman sitting with a friend in a corner of the club traditionally reserved for those seeking a new partner.

The girl was in her early twenties and had medium length brown hair. It was difficult to tell what her figure was like but her bizarre outfit was arousing a lot of attention. Precisely what was intended. She wore a long black coat, stockings, high heeled shoes, a white tuxedo-style shirt with a black bow tie. She seemed almost satanic. That really appealed to Bobby.

Their eyes met instantly. They both knew what the other was thinking. Bobby's pals were at the bar buying drinks. She loved to tease and flirt first – it was always much more fun. As her friends brought over the beers, Bobby turned her back to the girl in the corner. Every now and again she would sneak a glimpse of her.

The three friends supped greedily at their drinks. But Bobby's mind was on that girl, her vivid imagination working overtime. She was seeing her partly clothed on a bed. Vulnerable, excited, desperate. She wanted her. She would have her.

Bobby's sexual drive knew few boundaries. After all, here she was preparing for her next conquest, just a few hours after making brutal love to the girl she lived with. They had both arrived home early from college and neither of their two other flatmates were around. Bobby had grabbed her from behind in the kitchen and smothered her neck in kisses. At first her friend resisted, but Bobby was forceful and strong. Soon she was holding her down as she ground into her body. It was all over in minutes but that sexual drive was satisfied – at least for a while.

Back in the club, one of Bobby's friends was telling a crude joke. But they were all well aware that Bobby wasn't listening.

"She's all yours. Stop fantasising. Just get over there and pull her."

This was a Friday night in Brisbane, Australia. The whole town was out to enjoy the weekend. In these sunny climes, it was an excuse to commit a multitude of sins.

That was all the prompting Bobby needed. She could already feel her heart beat faster with excitement. A sexual thrill was rushing through her body, even though she hadn't spoken to the girl yet.

With black trousers and black tee-shirt, hobnail boots and an ever present pair of wire rimmed sunglasses, Bobby hardly exuded glamour. But, in a club like the Lew-Mors, no-one exactly dressed up for dinner.

The place was full of hard cases – all hoping to find a passion partner to share their bodies with. The dance floor was poorly lit. Soul music throbbed out of the loud speakers as couples gyrated together.

Bobby turned to face her admirer once more and their eyes met again. This time she did not hesitate. As she strode confidently over to the table, the girl squirmed expectantly in her seat. Lisa knew she was about to be swept off her feet.

The two talked a while. But deep, meaningful conversation was not exactly high on their list of priorities. They both knew what the other wanted.

That night was Friday the thirteenth of October, 1989.

Unlucky for some...

Lisa Ptaschinski curled up beside her sleeping lover. They had met just a few hours earlier, but she felt as if they had known each other for most of their life. On both her wrists were two tiny fresh scabs. Lisa looked at them and once more felt a rush to her brain as she remembered the sexual thrill she had experienced less than an hour before.

Within seconds of getting back to the apartment, these two strangers were exploring every inch of each other's bodies. After their first climax, both wanted more not less.

It was then that Lisa discovered her partner liked to play a game that even she had never tried before. As the two lovers lay back to recover from that first crescendo, they started to talk about blood. The taste of it. The smell of it. Even the colour of it. The more they talked about blood, the more excited Bobby became.

She was disarmingly frank: "I think I'm a vampire.

9

I can't resist blood. Its taste. Even its texture. Something inside me craves for it."

For a moment Lisa stopped and stared at Bobby. Then she felt really good. Her brand new lover was already revealing her inner-most thoughts to her. She wanted to please Bobby in every way.

Then, without a word, Lisa got up out of bed. A look of disappointment came over her lover's face. She presumed that she was getting up to go. But within moments Lisa had returned. Armed with a pointed kitchen knife she said simply, "Surprise..."

The tiny droplets of blood had to be literally coaxed out of Lisa's veins at first. But as her lover sucked harder, she felt a slight, but pleasurable pain from her wrist. Then the sucking got even stronger and she could feel the excitement building up inside. As a gesture of her passion, Lisa then stabbed gently at the vein on her other wrist and watched as her lover's face looked up at her, a tiny drip of blood dribbling down the side of the mouth as it curled into a smile of satisfaction, just like a cat who's got the cream.

Every now and again, Bobby kissed the tender flesh near Lisa's wrist, as if to assure her that she wasn't just into blood. But it was purely a token gesture for, within seconds, she would return to her favoured feast. She was captivated by Lisa's flawless complexion. Her skin really was as perfect as it looked. And it felt as smooth as syrup.

Lisa's legs were ever so slightly parted as Bobby sucked deeper and deeper into her. She could feel her breath speeding up. This was as exciting as those first days of sexual experimentation she had carried out at her convent school in Sydney. Lisa loved to feel she could constantly supply pleasure. It was almost more important to her than receiving satisfaction.

Now Bobby was gently moaning to herself – the excitement carrying a throaty noise that she emitted from within. It was a strange noise – sometimes high pitched, sometimes deep. A struggling noise.

Now the groans of pleasure were becoming louder as Lisa and Bobby moaned in unison. Bobby's sounds were sheer enjoyment. Lisa's were an extraordinary combination of pain and pleasure. The pain from the sucking, the pleasure came from giving.

As the pewter light of dawn shone through the opened window, the lovers continued, oblivious to the outside world. Locked in a dangerous, erotic world from which neither wanted to escape.

The Observer looked in at the scene. One lover lay on her back with her wrists flat on the bed as her partner feasted on the blood.

Neither of them noticed that a third party had entered the room. They were so wrapped up in the passion and the pain that they were oblivious to their surroundings.

"This is sick," muttered the Observer to herself, disgusted by the scene before her. Appalled. Yet fascinated. So she stayed in the room as the two lovers writhed, explored... and drank.

She wanted to stop them but something prevented her. Something made her stay there and witness this degradation. But she did not know what. And she did not know why...

Next morning, the two lovers held hands tightly at every available opportunity. With each squeezing motion, Lisa felt a slight twinge of pain in the scabs on her wrists. But it was a bearable pain. A sacrifice worth making for the one she adored.

As Bobby made breakfast, eight-year-old Tracey Wigginton appeared. She was a regular visitor to the flat. A child who's very presence was difficult to ever explain.

"What are you doing?" she asked in the blunt manner that only a child can get away with. "Are you in love?"

Bobby looked embarrassed. After all how could she explain her actions to an eight-year-old? Love is something that children have an instinct for – and they are usually right.

Little Tracey was desperate for love. She was brought up by her grandparents. But actually they were not really her mother's parents. To make matters worse, her step-grandfather abused her. Verbally by day and sexually by night. She had never forgotten how he used to get in her bed. Her life was messed up and she longed for security. That's why she often came into Bobby's life.

She missed out on real, normal emotions and could only relate to the harsh reality of a miserable, tortured environment. Now she was trying to make up for lost time... She soon disappeared from the apartment as quickly as she had arrived...

In less than twenty-four hours, Bobby and Lisa became close – close enough that Bobby decided to introduce Lisa to her great friends Tracey Waugh and Kim Jervis. Lisa was reluctant at first. After all, why should Bobby want her to meet two of her other women friends? They were probably lovers as well. She already felt pangs of jealousy. But Bobby was very forceful about it. "You'll love them. We can all have a good time together."

Lisa knew there was no way out – and maybe Bobby was right. When she wanted her own way, she usually got it.

As it happened, the foursome got on famously. Lisa's fears were unfounded. She started to not even care if Bobby had slept with any of them.

Tracey was twenty-four, an unemployed secretary. Dressed in a more feminine sort of way than her friends she seemed altogether a softer sort of character. Kim, the same age, was the only member of the group with a full-time job – as a photo processor. An attention grabbing kind of girl, she lapped up every word uttered by Bobby. Appreciative of the friendship and all that could lead to.

As they all drank their ice cool beer and swopped tales of life, Lisa happily acknowledged to herself that she was being swept up by Bobby and her friends. She'd always wanted a close circle of companions. Now she had found one.

Then Kim cracked a joke about blood. The table went silent. Bobby breathed – sharply. If they had been in a restaurant or bar, perhaps the atmosphere would have swept the conversation forward and everyone would have simply ignored the remark. But this scene was being played out in Kim's spotless suburban apartment in the Clayfield area of Brisbane. The atmosphere already bordered on the intimate. Now there was a chance to take it a stage further.

Bobby dimmed the lights and returned to the table where they were all sitting. She obviously had something important to contribute. Turning to her self-appointed protégé, Kim, she said coolly, "I want to scare you."

The other three sat in total silence.

Bobby removed her sunglasses and stared straight into their eyes, each in turn.

"She wanted to use her mind to make us compatible," explained Kim later. Quite simply, Bobby wanted to mind control her friends. She wanted to have the power over them that she lusted for constantly.

But first, she wanted to make Kim her "destroyer". That role meant Kim would become her disciple. Her messenger of all things.

The atmosphere was tightening by the second. Only Tracey remained somewhat sceptical but, as she was later to recall, "I was powerless to do anything. She had us in the palm of her hand."

Bobby was getting tough. "I have satanic powers and you will all become my disciples in time."

Lisa was fascinated. This sort of experience was what she had been looking for all her life. She was vulnerable. She desperately needed to be led – and Bobby was providing that lead.

Bobby got up from the table and picked a thick photo album out of a drawer in a nearby cupboard. She then spread the pictures across the table – about fifteen in all. They were all shots of headstones from nearby Harrisville Cemetery.

Bobby was convinced that each of the featured graves belonged to the devil. She talked of how they would come out at night and drive people to commit evil crimes.

"This is the way of the devil. You must realise this," she said, her strange voice veering from low, deep tones to a high, almost falsetto, shrill.

At no stage did any of the women even so much as question her claims – only Tracey had any doubts and she knew that now was not the time to air them.

It was only later that Tracey realised the significance of the fact that all the curtains in the apartment were closed, even though it was still daylight outside. The only explanation at the time was that Bobby was sensitive to sunlight. They had always been aware that she hated to go out in the day.

But Bobby was now concerned with bringing the conversation around to vampires.

"They do exist. I know. I am one," she insisted. "I need blood. I must have it."

The women watched in silence as Bobby went up to the fridge and took out a white butcher's plastic bag filled with blood. She devoured the entire contents, carelessly, or perhaps thirstily, spilling drops on her tee-shirt.

At that moment Tracey spotted the tiny scabs on Lisa's wrists and smiled a knowing smile. They were all becoming Bobby's disciples.

"I hunger for blood all the time. I need it in me," continued Bobby. No-one sitting there was in the slightest bit surprised.

Bobby openly revealed she had feasted on the blood of virtually every type of livestock animal. She was a regular at a handful of butchers' shops in the area

14

near her home. They learned not to raise an eyebrow at her bizarre requests for vast quantities of pig's blood. It had become a necessity as well as an obsession. Each day, she said, she had to drink blood.

But, animal blood did not really satisfy the appetite within her.

There was another, deeper need. And she wanted to feed it, to nurture it until it consumed her.

Every other person at that table had, at one time or other, given into Bobby's demands. They all had the tell-tale scabs on their wrists.

Bobby wanted more than just an ounce or two of blood this time. She wanted pints of the stuff. Human blood. And it had to be fresh because "that way it is cleaner and smoother and tastier."

She added chillingly, "By the time our man hits the ground his throat will be cut and he'll be dead."

Then she put a proposition to her friends. "Help me find a victim."

Ted Baldock was in a pretty good mood. It was Friday afternoon and soon he would be finished work for the weekend. A weekend that would no doubt include the two extremes of his life as a father-of-five – drunkeness and domesticity.

The weather was swelteringly hot. About ninety-five degrees in the shade. Brisbane in October was like a July day in New York. Sweat dripped off his lean shoulders.

For Ted it was harder than most. No air-conditioned office for him to sit back in. His workplace was the roads of the city and his "typewriter" was a pneumatic drill that throbbed and hammered into the sun-baked tarmac.

Ted had struggled hard for nearly thirty years to support his huge family. He and wife Elaine had found it pretty difficult at times. But they had survived all the ups and downs that married life could throw at them. Ted had a thick skin that proved ideal for a lifelong marriage. Now, at forty-seven, he was starting to look forward to retirement, a pension and the blissful relaxation after years of providing. Maybe a bit of fishing, probably a fair deal of boozing. But no pressures. No demands.

His body ached with exhaustion from the hard week he had endured. Ted was not your macho-muscle man like many of his colleagues on the road repair squad for Brisbane City Council. He was a modest sort of fellow. Not prone to even taking his shirt off in public – let alone flaunting his biceps. Elaine and many of his friends at home in the West End district of Brisbane were always telling Ted not to overdo it.

As he jerked the drill into place for the last time on the roadside, his thoughts were rapidly wandering to the weekend. If he'd known what lay ahead, he'd have stopped thinking there and then...

The Holden Commodore came to a halt outside Lisa's home in Leichardt. She heard her lover sound the horn twice. As the pretty brown haired girl looked out of the window of the tiny box-built house, their eyes locked. It was almost the same feeling as that first time they had met and seduced each other just seven days earlier.

Landlady Wendy Sugden was curious. She felt a great deal of responsibility for Lisa since the day, just five weeks earlier, they had met at Ipswich General Hospital. Lisa was the patient, and Wendy her nurse had taken her under her wing. They struck up a real friendship.

Lisa looked upon Wendy as a mother figure. Always there when she was needed. Providing a vital support to lean on. Wendy and her husband Wayne had an ordinary little house, but it was clean and tidy and the nearest thing to home that Lisa had ever known. When she told Wendy about Bobby, the nurse frowned. She sounded like trouble but then Lisa was always going to be a problem person.

As Lisa skipped out of the front door to her waiting admirer, she thought back to that first night of outrageous passion. Then, as if to reassure herself, she scratched the top of the tiny scab on her left wrist – just to make sure that every moment of lust they shared had actually happened.

The two lovers kissed deeply within moments of Lisa getting in the car. Lisa could feel the body heat oozing off her partner. If it hadn't still been daylight they might have made love there and then.

Wendy watched everything from a ground floor window, saddened by the inevitability that it would all end in tears… or worse. She'd seen it all before. Lisa's life revolved around disastrous relationships.

Lisa looked at her lover for a moment as they untangled themselves. A new, darker midnight black hairstyle made the features far more severe than when they last met. She was looking more and more like the vampire she had convinced herself she was.

Lisa did not notice the bulge in Bobby's black jacket pocket. She could only think forward to another night of sex. She knew there was going to be a real "treat" in store for Bobby this time.

It was a thirty minute drive to the other girls' homes. During that time, Bobby kept saying how hungry she was. How she was looking forward to feasting. Her appetite for blood had definitely increased.

Her thirst would soon be quenched.

But first, they had to pick up Kim and Tracey from their apartments in Clayfield.

Kim and Tracey jumped into the car, chatting rapidly, eager expectation etched on their faces. Once again, Lisa failed to notice another bulge – this time in Kim's pocket.

If she had looked inside that pocket, she would have seen a ninja butterfly pocket knife with a 10cm blade. Kim had bought it in the nearby Fortitude Valley army disposal shop after they'd discussed their plans...

Ted Baldock was back at the council changing rooms stripping off his filthy work clothes before showering in preparation for a Friday night on the town. Like millions of manual workers the world over, Ted took a great pride in dressing up whenever he went out. It was as if he longed for the clean cut life of an office worker. Wearing a smart pair of slacks and a newly starched shirt was a real pleasure.

For him, the grass was always greener on the other side. There were many things he longed for in life.

As he washed himself under a piping hot cascade of water, he felt the energy returning to those tired bones. Ted was looking forward with relish to the first glass of beer of the day. He felt he deserved to treat himself.

For the previous six Fridays, Ted, sometimes with Elaine in tow, had become a regular of the Caledonian Club at Kangaroo Point. It was a rough and ready joint but Ted liked the atmosphere and no-one stopped you drinking however much you wanted. You could sup to your heart's content, and no-one gave a damn. So long as you didn't puke on the floor, that is.

He'd discovered the place after being taken there by a workmate. It was a great escape from the tedium of a week spent working on the roads and watching mindless TV at his West End home.

As he strolled the short distance from the council changing rooms to the Caledonian, he could literally smell the beer in his nostrils. It was a good feeling. He was going to have a great time tonight. He could feel it in his blood.

The girls had all agreed that the Lew-Mors was the perfect place to start their night out, to savour the anticipation. But Bobby was anxious now. Counting the minutes. It had to be midnight before they could strike. It was no use before then. It had to be just like the Dracula books she used to read so avidly when she was at school.

Instead of beers and spirits, the four friends ordered champagne. This evening was special. Soon they would have something extraordinary to celebrate.

The club manageress was astounded. "They were buzzing with excitement," she said when she looked back on that fateful night. And some of the regulars thought the weird foursome were planning an orgy.

As they sat at a table just by the DJs booth, the girls drank a toast... to blood. The blood of a human who still had no idea he was to become their victim.

Ted had spent hours indulging in his favourite game – darts. After a few beers, he was taking on everyone and losing. But no-one minded, Ted was a good loser. Always good for a laugh.

He ended the evening holding up the bar. Or perhaps the bar was holding up him. Either way the two inanimate objects were getting along just fine. This sort of vast beer consumption was nothing new for Ted and the barmen were happy to keep on feeding him alcohol because he wasn't making a pest of himself.

Every now and again he would talk to an acquaintance about the meaning of life. But it would only be a passing gesture – nothing of a seriously friendly nature. No one in the bar that evening was a great friend of Ted Baldock.

It was getting towards midnight and that meant it was time for all the Teds of Brisbane to get on their merry way home. As last orders were called, he persuaded a barman to give him one last refill. He downed it quickly, stumbled out into the balmy night, and concentrated, in vain, on finding his way home.

He knew that Elaine – while a loving, caring and patient wife – would not tolerate his non appearance, whatever the excuse.

Across town, Bobby, Lisa, Kim and Tracey were

finishing off their second bottle of bubbly.

"What are you celebrating? Love and marriage?" asked one hostess.

The four giggled in expectation. Bobby admired the girl's shapely legs.

"Wouldn't you like to know sweetheart," she cooed seductively.

Lisa felt a twinge of jealousy. Bobby had the sort of eyes that probed everywhere. Every time a pretty girl passed by, she could sense Bobby's eyes upon their body, sizing up the sex content. She consoled herself by remembering she was hers – even if Bobby did fantasise about the size of the waitress' breasts.

The champagne was now really having an effect and all four felt the headiness unique to France's favourite drink. They felt sensuous, carefree, daring. There was a buzz in the air. Bobby kept talking about her hunger. Her appetite. Her obsession. Blood.

She was the one person at that table who really knew what lay ahead...

Outside the Lew-Mors, the hunt was about to begin. It was dead on midnight. Everything was perfect. Bobby had the expectant look of someone about to win a huge prize.

"I'll drive. Then you can pick one," said Lisa as they got into Bobby's car. At first, Bobby was reluctant to allow Lisa to drive. She was the "man" in their relationship and it was her car. But then she saw the sense in what Lisa was saying. No-one else could choose the victim except Bobby.

To begin with, they drove at a steady 30 mph towards the Botanic Gardens district of the city. It was a lively night-time area – perfect for what they had in mind. For ten minutes they drove around the streets hovering outside the nightclubs and pubs, but there was no suitable prey.

Then they headed for the New Farm Park area and they soon spotted a lonely figure staggering in a zigzag along the pavement. The Commodore slowed down. This was what they were looking for.

The man turned and faced straight into the car's headlights. He looked perfect.

But then another man appeared from an alleyway. Two was too many. Too difficult to handle. They had to be patient.

They drove on, disappointed.

Bobby did not feel like being patient. She was hungry. She couldn't wait. It was past midnight. Feeding time.

Then they decided to head for Kangaroo Point. A last resort. There had to be someone around.

The night sounded empty and strangely quiet. It was almost as if a massive storm had passed and left in its wake an eerie, dead calm. A thin, motionless fog hung near the water's edge, catching the silver light of the moon.

Sprawled face down on the pavement lay Ted Baldock. He wasn't actually out cold. But he was definitely suffering. He blinked and waited in the hope that things would come back into focus. He inhaled deep breaths of air to try to compose himself. He had to make it home to Elaine and the children.

Gradually his vision began to clear and he hauled himself up from the ground grasping on to a lampost for support. As he clambered to his feet, the headlights of an approaching car shone fiercely in his eyes.

All he could see was a blur of light. He wasn't even sure if it was moving at first. It was only when the vehicle got closer that he could make out a car. For a moment, Ted forgot where he was or how he had got there. He tried to concentrate and was pleasantly surprised. It wasn't that hard after all. That brief "rest" on the sidewalk had definitely helped recover his senses.

The car was getting closer. Ted was trying to get his mind around what all this meant. Maybe he could thumb a lift or maybe it was a taxi. He felt in his

21

pockets. He had some money. He tried to flag it down.

In the pitch black, Ted couldn't begin to even guess the size and shape of the occupants – it was all too much for his addled brain to cope with. But being a friendly drunk leaning against a lamp-post, he could not imagine their intentions were anything other than honourable.

"You want a ride?" a woman's voice beckoned. Kim and Bobby had got out of the car. They felt they should guide him to the vehicle.

Ted did not hesitate.

He hauled himself off the lamp-post and headed, unsteadily, in the direction of the car. One step at a time at first. Then, as his confidence grew, he began to walk more steadily. The couple opened the passenger door and another female voice beckoned.

"Come on in."

Then one of them helped Ted in. He found himself hemmed between two attractive looking long haired women in their early twenties – and he wasn't complaining. The whole thing seemed so unreal.

He could only just make out the hair of one women in front and the short back and sides of the female driver.

Ted was sobering up now. These girls were out for some fun. He couldn't believe his luck. They stroked his body through his clothes, kissed his ear and nibbled his neck. He felt himself harden at the prospect of all these girls. Who knows? Maybe he'd get a ride home as part of the bargain?

"You want to have some *real* fun?" asked one girl. Ted didn't even need to bother replying. There was only one real answer. He had money. But he wasn't even sure if they wanted it. They just seemed to want him.

The car stopped just near the prestigious South Brisbane Yacht Club. But it was way past those yachtsmen's bedtimes and the place was silent and locked up for the night.

Midnight had come and gone and Bobby was hungry. Very hungry.

She told a dazed Ted to go down to the river's edge with her to sort out the money and then the girls would join him. This really was turning out to be Ted's lucky night.

It was the first time he had tried to walk since struggling to the car just a few minutes earlier. Yet, now he had a fresh motive and, although still very drunk, he had purpose in his walk. He knew where he was going and he thought he knew precisely what he was about to get from these girls.

As Ted approached the river's edge, Bobby went back to the car. What little light there was disappeared from view. There had been a streetlight some half a mile away but now it was gone.

Splinters of wood that had been blown off the trees by recent gales crackled beneath his feet.

Back in the Holden Commodore, Kim and Tracey were scared.

"Let's just leave him there," they both pleaded. But Lisa and Bobby had other plans.

Just moments before, they had all watched the pathetic figure of Ted walking down to the riverside to prepare for his night of passion. But they all knew that he was there only to provide the thrills for them.

Bobby was angry with Kim and Tracey. After all, they had all agreed on this "celebration". Now there was a break down of discipline in the ranks. But the two mutineers refused to budge.

In an act of defiance Kim flung her knife on to the front arm rest of the car. Bobby scowled at her, then grabbed it and stormed off.

On the riverbank, Ted stripped off completely. Despite all the drink he had consumed he had the good sense to put his wallet and keys in one of his shoes. The last thing he wanted was to lose anything valuable.

Then he sat – a slightly ludicrous figure – naked on

23

the bank and waited for his women to appear.

It was pitch black and the only sound was the river lapping gently on the bank. Every now and again there would be a plop in the water as an insect hit the surface.

A voice then told Ted to move to a clearer strip of river bank just a few yards upstream. It was Bobby's voice – but it had become high pitched and difficult to distinguish. Also, it was said with such command that anyone would have felt obliged to obey it.

Ted turned to see who it was but there was no-one there. He just presumed that the order was a guarantee of what was to come. He readily obeyed – convinced that his happy moment was fast approaching.

As he walked the short distance, he spotted what he thought was his credit card. In the poor light, Ted did not even check to see if it was actually his.

Instead, he just dropped it into one of his shoes for safe-keeping. He neatly laid out his clothes in a pile. It seemed as sensible a place as any to put your valuables when you are about to indulge in some casual sex with girls you have never met before.

"He's going to be too strong for just me." Bobby turned to Lisa. "You've got to come."

Lisa hesitated for a moment and then looked into those piercing eyes and felt obliged to aid her lover. She knew exactly what was intended. She had encouraged it because she wanted Bobby to be satisfied. She could not retreat now. They were lovers and you always do whatever your lover wants.

The two girls in the back looked stunned, but they kept their thoughts to themselves. They were now shivering with fright, holding each other other for comfort. Desperate to escape from this nightmare and return to reality.

Bobby grasped Lisa's hand. That slight pain from the scab on her vein returned as if to remind her of what was to come. They walked gingerly around the back of the yacht club to where Ted was waiting patiently.

They were systematically holding their breath and then releasing short bursts of air, so as not to make much noise. Lisa's hand was hot and clammy. Bobby's was cool, almost ice cool, considering the heat of the night. They both realised one thing – the element of surprise was essential...

Ted was getting irritated. He wanted sex and it was not forthcoming. He was fed up with sitting on that riverbank. Although his vision was adapting well to the poor light, he failed to see the two figures approaching him from behind.

Bobby and Lisa could now clearly see Ted's back in the moonlight. He had that slightly loose skin that many men get as they approach their fifties. He was crouching, awkwardly swinging from side to side. Occasionally, Ted would shake his head to force himself awake after nodding off to sleep.

Each time he fell into a slumber, he would begin to dream vivid visions – only to snap himself awake. He was waiting for an orgy to begin and those dreams were becoming so daunting.

Bobby had a shiny object in each hand and Lisa could see in her eyes that same look that came over her whenever they were about to make love.

They stopped some yards short of Ted and quietly removed their clothes. They wanted to guarantee that Ted would not struggle until they were ready to feast. The sight of two lithe, female bodies in the dark would leave him in no doubt of their intent.

Ted shifted his position slightly as the two lovers approached. He looked behind and could just make out their naked bodies. He glanced at them before looking out to the river once more. He could not believe his luck – two nubile, young girls. Wait till he told his mates at work about this. He was happy to wait for them to come to him – after all he was going to pay. If he had stared a little harder he would have seen, rather than felt, the first frenzy of knife stabs that were soon to rain down on him from Bobby's hands.

Bobby was shaking with need. She needed blood. Here she was, about to kill as she stood in the dark on the river bank. Something inside was urging her to murder an innocent man.

She was going to kill. There was nothing she could do to stop it. The more she thought of her own cruel upbringing, the more she failed to shame herself about committing murder. She could not control her hunger.

Many people thought that murder was a sin. Bobby reckoned she knew otherwise. Some were born with a taste for blood. Others had it instilled in them. Bobby always claimed she drank the blood of live goats when she ran away from her cruel "grandparents" at the age of just 15.

But God had made each man as he was and Bobby had been chosen to kill. It was all part of the masterplan. In Bobby's eyes, the only sin was to kill when your lover did not approve of the victim. But they had all chosen this victim together. They all knew what Bobby wanted. That gave her the licence to kill...

Standing there, watching by the river's edge was The Observer. She was shocked. How could Bobby kill? She should be ashamed by her terrible actions. Surely it was not too late to stop? But the beast within Bobby would always ignore the truth. And The Observer knew that really. She was powerless to stop the onslaught. It was out of her control.

As Bobby got closer, the dead calm returned. Like beasts prowling in the night, they slowed down as they approached their victim. Then they paused momentarily, waiting for the perfect moment.

The Observer was now pleading, begging Bobby to stop. Stop now.

Bobby knew what she was being told. She knew that what she was doing was wrong. But the urge from within was still too strong to resist.

"Stop. Stop. Stop." The Observer screamed. "This is crazy. Insane. Get ahold of yourself..." But the words were soon lost in the wind. Never to return.

Bobby let out one long pent up breath. Her family had never really taught her that killing was wrong. But then they were not a proper family. They had never drawn the moral lines that every child so desperately needs. Instead, she had been beaten and abused whenever she committed a wrong doing. No-one ever explained why. Often Bobby would be locked in her room as a child and visited by her grandfather when he wanted to hurt her or have sex with her – or worse.

On other occasions, Bobby's family could look straight through her, as if she didn't even exist. They never provided any warmth, comfort or security. Instead, she was told how bad she was. How the very mention of her name would make them feel sick. How she was a lazy, no-good, evil little brat.

They would take out the belt and thrash her. Now, she wanted to show them, show them all just how evil she really was.

But Bobby was sure her horrible family would understand why she could not control herself on this night. They might not forgive her, but they would inspire her to commit the deed. Bobby reckoned she knew where all those relatives would have ended up – and it certainly was not heaven.

Then the girls pounced.

Ted buckled and thrashed as he fell onto his back but he couldn't shake off the assault. He no longer had the strength. He gurgled and spluttered as his mouth filled with blood and rapidly his convulsions became less violent before fading altogether.

Fifteen times Bobby plunged her two knives into Ted's shoulders. A soft ripping sound came with each stab. One after the other they rained in on him. The blood seeping out of each wound. Bobby was now pomelling the knives, rather than grinding them, into his body. It was the same action as if she were thumping her fists on a table. She could not stop. Ted lay motionless on his back, but it didn't stop Bobby. She attacked his neck and chest just to make doubly sure there was no more life left in the mutilated corpse.

In a way this part of the attack was even more frenzied. Ted could not fight back and that invited a more ferocious response.

All the time she was stabbing with the knife she thought of her family. Of how she had begged them for love. But none of them would forgive her for inflicting herself upon them.

Ted was now a tangled mound of a body, crumpled on the grassy embankment. With the ninja knife, Bobby coldly and calmly slit Ted's throat from ear to ear. Lisa watched in fascination. She was so excited by the sight of her lover's naked body. She knew all about her urges and she wanted to see those cravings satisfied.

Bobby crouched over the body and began to lick and drink the blood that poured from the victim's throat. More memories came flooding back. Bobby recalled how she had discovered her grandmother was not her real blood relative. How she was told her mother had abandoned her. None of her seven brothers and sisters were related to her. Life had been one long betrayal.

No-one could be trusted.

She swirled her tongue around the inside of the gaping wound, trying to devour every last morsel. But there was more than enough there.

She pushed the severed head further back to expose the throat wound even further – giving her more access to the blood. Now she was devouring the flesh like a shark in a feeding frenzy. The skin ripped open like a PVC dustbin bag when it's been over-filled.

Bobby then turned to Lisa. She had a lip curling smile that showed she had fed sufficiently – for the moment.

Businessman Scott Evans Gamble was sitting on the opposite side of the river bank when he heard the groans. A wry smile came to his face as they grew in sound to reach an ecstatic peak of what he presumed was sexual climax.

Lisa was now breathing in short and sharp gasps. She watched admiringly as her lover washed her body in the warm river water. Calmly, Bobby splashed water over her breasts and legs as if washing in a shower or bath.

She was only allowed one shallow bath a week at home. This was fantastic. A whole river to lose oneself in. A torrent of never ending water deep enough to swim in.

Once, at home, she was banned from eating at mealtime because she urinated in the bath. Now she could do it to her heart's content and no-one could stop her.

Soon the blood marks were washed away, but Bobby still had some other unfinished business to attend to. She strolled naked to the river bank where she picked up both the knives used in the killing and washed them lovingly in the river before carrying them back on to the river bank where the mutilated torso lay twisted on its back by the muddy verge.

Both lovers stood there for a moment in the darkness, enveloped by the pungent aroma of blood. The smell was particularly strong when Bobby's breath wafted towards Lisa.

She could feel the globules of blood and flesh mixed together after becoming caught between her teeth. Using the tip of her tongue, Bobby tried to push them out from between the gaps.

Her first real taste of blood had come when she was swept up into a witch's coven near her home in Rock Hampton. She had been fascinated by the man and wife, whom the locals used to refer to as the witches.

They offered her a place to sleep. It was nicer than her foster parents home. They often made sacrifices of animals like goats. They extended her education... in blood.

Bobby put on the jeans and tee-shirt that were her regular "uniform" around town. She was remarkably calm. Spent and satisfied like a lover who has just climaxed.

They walked back towards the car... hand in hand.

Watching them from nearby was The Observer. She was astounded. How could anyone do such a thing? A feeling of utter contempt and disgust came over her.

She kept repeating those eight words to herself. "How could anyone do such a dreadful thing," over and over. But she was powerless to act.

"I have just feasted. I have just feasted," Bobby screamed again and again as they drove the 30 minute trip back to their homes.

The journey was truly bizarre. Tracey Waugh, close to tears, sat soberly in a corner of the back seat, terrified to speak. No-one said much. All three women later recalled how they smelt the overwhelming aroma of the blood on Bobby's breath. It was pungent and nauseous. They said Bobby looked and behaved as if she had just enjoyed a three-course dinner.

Two boys were sitting in the back of a police squad car, shaking with fear. But this was not the fear of arrest. This was the shock of just having found the mutilated body of Ted Baldock.

Just a few yards away, behind the impressive facade of the South Brisbane Yacht Club, Detective Constable Danny Murdoch grimaced. He was a well-built cop with the likeable smile of a perennial optimist; but even his cheerful outlook on life was strained to breaking point by the sight that greeted him.

"The guy looks like he got the ultimate head job," said Detective Constable Barry Deveney. Nobody laughed. It was six a.m. on Saturday, October 21, and every detective called to the scene that day had been dragged in on a day off to join the murder inquiry.

The forensic team were already examining the area around the body for any minute clues. Murdoch leant down to examine Ted's clothes, which were still in a neat pile.

Policemen were cordoning off the area with white plastic tape. A small crowd had gathered just a few yards from the yacht club.

As the coroners' officers lifted the body into a zippered plastic corpse bag, some of the crowd grimaced. But they still continued to stare, fascinated by the macabre scene. They were detached from the emotion of losing a loved one. Just curious to take a look. To tell their friends they saw a body on the riverbank. It would be something to brag about when the conversation ran dry in the bars and pubs of Brisbane that night.

Murdoch picked up Ted's scruffy shoes and heard the unmistakable, jangling noise of a set of keys. He reached inside to take them out and found a credit card. The name on it clearly read: Tracey Wigginton. That was Bobby's real name.

Detective Sergeant Glenn Burton, 40, was looking forward to a nice family Saturday at home. He had almost finished washing the car with his three children. And, unlike most husbands, he was more than happy to accompany his wife and kids to the supermarket.

Their home at Wynnum was a picturesque spot right on the bay. Beautiful views, beautiful weather. What more could a man ask for?

Glenn was putting the finishing touches to his car when he heard the phone. It was still early, so he knew it was unlikely to be family or friends. On occasions like this it was tempting not to answer or let one of the family say he was out. But Glenn Burton was not that kind of guy.

He was a straight man who knew that a policeman was never really off duty. He was just "resting" between cases.

It was, therefore, hardly surprising when one of the kids said the call was for him. His assignment was to go and arrest the owner of that credit card.

Within minutes, Glenn was heading for Enoggera and the home of Tracey Wigginton. The police had a simple theory. Ted was murdered by a girlfriend and her other lover.

The clues were pretty well there for everyone to see. The tyre marks from the car. The footsteps of two other people besides Ted. The ferocity of the stab wounds implied a woman had stood by and watched while her lover/husband carried out the killing.

As Glenn and five colleagues walked calmly up the stairs of the apartment block where Tracey Wigginton lived, it all seemed pretty clear cut.

Bobby was watching television. She had not slept well – mainly because Lisa did not stay the night with her. Bobby's three flat mates were sitting around drinking coffee, relaxing. It was a Saturday morning and they were all taking it easy.

There was a knock at the door. It was a firm, officious knock and Bobby knew instantly who it was. She went to answer it.

"Tracey Wigginton?" asked Glenn Burton.

"Bobby" had gone back into the sub-conscious of

Tracey. She had taken on her real-life persona once more. There was no more eight-year-old Tracey to show innocence. Even The Observer was gone.

They had all returned into the mind of 23-year-old sheet metal college student Tracey Wigginton. The moment the police came calling, her four-way personality had dispersed. She could no longer hide behind those weird characters.

They were a part of her alter-ego. Not even the dominating force of Bobby could help. Tracey was going to have to cope with this living nightmare herself. There was no-one else to turn to. Bobby never existed. Little Tracey never existed. The Observer was only her common sense telling her, warning her, what she was doing.

But this was reality. A reality that would cost Tracey Wigginton her liberty for the horrendous crime she had committed.

Bobby may have been in charge when those knives rained down on Ted Baldock's back. Bobby drank the blood and virtually severed the head to get more blood. Bobby seduced and lured Lisa Ptaschinski into joining those evil forces. But they'd all gone now, crawled back into the dark recesses of Tracey's troubled brain.

Tracey knew that as she opened that door, but she did not flinch. Her cold eyes stared confidently ahead as she faced Detective Sergeant Glenn Burton.

However, none of this was familiar territory for Glenn Burton. He still thought he was interviewing the estranged lover of Ted Baldock – not a multipersonality lesbian vampire with a lust for blood and murder.

The real Tracey Wigginton was a cold calculating killer, who knew her legal rights. She may have gone along quietly to the police station but she was not about to confess her evil deeds to Glenn.

Kim Jervis and Tracey Waugh were worried. Neither of them had managed much sleep that night. Their

33

consciences were beginning to get the better of them. And to make matters worse, they had heard about Tracey Wigginton's arrest.

Waugh was the most terrified. At her flat in Clayfield, she cried herself to sleep many hours after the killing of Ted Baldock. She really never wanted any part in the horrific murder.

Jervis – who lived in a separate apartment, also in Clayfield – was equally scared. But she had even more reason. Her knife had been used by Tracey Wigginton in the frenzied attack. She knew it was only a matter of time before the police came looking for her.

Ptaschinski was an all together different animal. She saw the killing and encouraged Wigginton by not trying to stop her murdering Ted Baldock.

To Lisa it had all been a game, a joke. Even now, with the reality of the situation fast encroaching, she still thrilled at the very thought of her love for Bobby.

In Bobby, she had a strong lover with whom she was willing to do anything. As she later told psychiatrist Dr Terry Mulholland: "If you are going out with someone you do whatever you can to please them."

The brutal sex. The blood letting. The murder. They were all just part of the thrill of an intense relationship for Lisa. She said later she was infatuated. Obsessive love can cloud judgement. Lisa had lost touch with reality for eight torrid days.

Now she had to try to work out if she knew the real Tracey Wigginton. Not Bobby the he-man, not eight-year-old Tracey and certainly not The Observer. Lisa needed to be able to predict Tracey's behaviour but she never somehow managed that. The fact remained that she couldn't tell if Tracey had started singing to police.

Tracey had had an in-built fear of looking at herself in the mirror since her earliest years. She hated to look at herself. Her confidence was shattered by the cruel jibes of her step family. She convinced herself she was ugly and never even bothered to make the effort to smarten herself up.

Her family would frequently punish her for not brushing her hair before school. Tracey began to believe that mirrors were evil objects which reflected her true self – something she could not face up to. Maybe her family were right? Perhaps she was evil? But she didn't really care.

Now here were the police joining a long list of her castigators. She knew just how to act. Calm and detached.

Glenn Burton was puzzled. Having raided Wigginton's flat, it had become blatantly obvious that she was a lesbian living in what locals call "a dyke's commune". Even when officers later returned to her flat and found a black cape and other satanic style clothing, they were still baffled.

"After all, black is a trendy colour these days. To link it with vampires seemed somewhat excessive," explained Glenn later.

Glenn wanted to know why poor old Ted had stripped down for sex with her by the riverbank. Wigginton was not telling. Her only response was no response. She simply refused to speak.

Glenn feared this was going to be a tough case to crack. He stood over Wigginton as she sat at one of the two desks in the white-walled dayroom at Wooloon Gabba police station.

As the warm midday sunlight dazzled through the office windows, Tracey blinked and squirmed in her seat. It was not the presence of the officers that bothered her, she just felt uncomfortable in direct sunlight. It was a bit like her fear of mirrors and it fueled the vampire involvement that scandalised Brisbane.

Ironically, on that day, she was relatively well dressed with a pretty white blouse and jeans. Despite the severe haircut she still retained a certain femininity about her.

She'd been there for more than four hours and all they'd got so far was her name and address. But Glenn was still under the impression they needed to find a boyfriend.

The idea of a woman killing at random just did not add up. Men were the cold, calculating murderers. They were the ones who often picked out complete strangers as their victims. No woman could commit such a brutal crime as this. Surely?

Tracey Waugh couldn't take the pressure any more. She had always been the least likely member of the group. Never quite as keen as the others. Always holding back. At one stage her fears led her to believe that Wigginton planned to make her the next blood victim. Waugh was the one who most shied away from the actual murder. She was the one who was close to tears in the back of the car the previous night.

She was painfully aware that Wigginton was sizing her up, imagining the taste of her blood. Or maybe she was lusting after her for sex as well?

Waugh pleaded with Jervis to turn themselves in. As they sat agonising at Jervis's tiny apartment, the two women became increasingly agitated by their situation.

They could not quite believe all this was happening. Would Wigginton incriminate them?

But at the home of Wendy and Wayne Sugden, Lisa was starting to wonder as well. One moment she imagined that Bobby/Tracey would walk through the door and sweep her off her feet. The next moment she recalled the look of terror on the face of that victim as he was punctured to death.

The Sugdens knew that there was something bothering Lisa. They wanted the truth and they were prepared to coax it out of her. Earlier in the week, she had told them all about Tracey. They were worried.

Not only about the lesbian relationship but the fact that Lisa was so easily lead. She liked to be dominated and Tracey was definitely doing that.

They were especially concerned when Lisa told them about the blood lust and Tracey's claims to be a vampire. Now, the look on Lisa's pathetic face said it all. She seemed to be in a trance. Out of touch with everyone and everything.

But that didn't stop the Sugdens being shocked when she blurted out "Tracey's murdered someone."

Wendy Sugden was stunned. At first, she failed to comprehend the full meaning of this statement.

"Was it an animal?"

Lisa just muttered: "A man."

Wendy and her husband were sickened by what they heard. But they knew instinctively it must be true. They had little difficulty in convincing Lisa to turn herself into the police that afternoon.

The same dilemma ultimately sealed all their fates.

For less than an hour later, Tracey and Kim also walked into the same police station. Until their appearance, Wigginton had sat in stony silence, refusing to co-operate.

If the others had not come forward then maybe Tracey would never have been convicted.

By one a.m. the next morning, an exhausted Glenn Burton left the station for his bayside home having solved what was probably the most horrific killing ever committed by women.

In October, 1990, Tracey Wigginton pleaded guilty to the murder of Ted Baldock at Brisbane Supreme Court and was jailed for life.

In February, 1991, Lisa Ptaschinski was found guilty of murder and also sentenced to life.

At the same hearing, Kim Jervis was convicted of manslaughter and jailed for eight years.

Tracey Waugh was cleared of murder and freed.

2

Twin Obsession

It was hardly a grand affair – as weddings go. But then Graham and Gillian Philpott would not have wanted it any other way really.

As they walked out of the quiet suburban registry office into the autumn sunlight, they felt a sense of relief that they had finally done it.

After all, they knew each other pretty well, having lived together for five years. Hardly a sin, but for most of that time, bank manager Graham had pretended to be married to avoid the bigoted gossip that their neighbours loved to indulge in.

It just would not do for a 45 year-old, recently divorced father-of-three to be setting up home with the pretty 21 year-old clerk from his branch of a major high-street bank.

For Mungo Park Way, near Orpington, in Kent, was one of those sort of places. Lots of net curtains and perfectly mowed lawns. A veneer of respectability hiding a multitude of sins.

Graham Philpott's house was a classic example of early 1970s architecture. Functional, practical and entirely lacking in style. But then it did have a built in garage – and that was very important in Mungo Park Way.

Now Graham and Gillian had got married at last. With two failed marriages behind him, Graham wanted to start afresh. Gillian made him feel so much younger.

For her part, she'd put her spotless past on the line to marry a man more than twice her age. Not surprisingly, her parents did not entirely approve of the match.

Her father, retired special branch police detective Leslie Smoothy, was philosophical. "They seem happy," he observed dryly. Gillian was old enough to make up her own mind whom she should marry.

In her stunning off-the-shoulder wedding dress complete with lace veil, she really looked the part as they left the ceremony to a cheery send off from a handful of friends and relatives.

She was an attractive woman in a chiselled sort of way, possessing one of those faces with sharp features that people either love or hate. There was no middle-of-the-road reaction about Gillian.

At work, she was always immaculately dressed and bubbled enthusiasm wherever she went. Her gregarious behaviour certainly caught the eye of her colleague Graham. Balding and nearly always wearing the same style of grey flannel suit in the office, he looked the archetypal bank manager.

Within a few months of Gillian joining the bank, they had become a definite couple. Soon, they were openly holding hands and kissing and cuddling as they travelled to and from the City by commuter train each day. No-one objected so long as it did not interfere with their work – and Graham made sure of that.

Now – five years later – she had actually persuaded him to marry her. They had learned to live together. To accept each other's habits. To enjoy each other's company. They were probably much better prepared than most other couples. The marriage meant something really special to them despite having been live-in lovers for so long. They wanted the ceremony to be an occasion to remember. A time of great happiness.

So when Gillian's sister Janet turned up at their house just a few days before the wedding in tears, it pained them both to see her in such distress. It was only natural that they should offer her a shoulder to cry on.

Janet had just finished a particularly turbulent love affair and her life seemed in tatters. She did the only natural thing – and turned to her twin sister for comfort.

They were not absolutely identical. But the facial resemblances were startling similar. The nose, the eyes, the mouth, the shape of the face. If you met the sister you did not know in the street, you would be sure you had seen her before.

They did not dress identically because they abhorred the habitual obligation that so many twins seem under. They were individuals and they wanted to be treated as such.

If anything, being twin sisters had made Gillian and Janet more determined to succeed on their own. Throughout their childhood, they had suffered the pressure of always being expected to perform like circus clowns. People tried to make one person out of two. It was so infuriating they promised each other they would never treat their own children that way.

It was no surprise, then, that they went their own separate ways. Even so, despite the distance they kept from each other, Janet still managed to have exactly the same job as her sister, for the same bank – but at a different branch.

Perhaps that was why the guests at the wedding that day were not the least bit shocked to see Janet sitting with her sister and brand new husband in the back of their chauffeur driven limousine as it drove off to London Airport.

Earlier, Gillian had been relieved when her husband had put up no resistance to her suggestion that Janet should accompany them on their honeymoon to beautiful Bali. It wouldn't marr the holiday. In fact, she thought, it would be quite nice to have some female company. Graham could be awfully staid at times. And Bali sounded like such a wonderful place. Situated just south of Indonesia and west of Java, it really promised to be the trip of a lifetime.

Graham Philpott had been bemused by his wife's suggestion at first. Slightly irritated that the romantic holiday was going to be with someone else. But, when she had explained the anguish her sister was going through, he thought it would be heartless to object. In any case, Janet was going to return to London after two weeks – to leave them with a full week to themselves.

As they sat together chatting on the flight to paradise,

Graham studied Janet more closely. They really were identical twins in more ways than he had at first realised. Talking to Janet was just like talking to a more sophisticated version of Gillian. She seemed less hard-faced. More demure. More ladylike in the way she dressed and behaved. He examined all the features of her body. It was her eyes that struck him most. They were so inviting. She would look at him in such a way that he felt as if she were reading his mind.

Janet possessed something her sister lacked. He wasn't entirely sure what it was. But he thought he might like to find out.

Graham and Gillian had the honeymoon suite. It was a sumptuous place. Servants at your beck and call. Food, drink, sunshine, even massages on tap.

At night the two newly weds walked barefoot along the endless palm-fringed beaches, golden sand scrunching beneath their feet.

Bali has been called "The Morning of the World." An enchanting island, it is without doubt, one of the most magical places on earth. Scattered between the trees are tiny villages where craftsmen build countless temples in honour of their gods. Every night, after the sun goes down, traditional Balinese dancing takes place. The perfect place to relax. The perfect place for a honeymoon.

There was so much for the newly-weds to do.

Then there was Janet. She was always around. Laughing. Joking. Playing a hostess-type role to the two lovers. Whenever she felt in the way, she would disappear, sensing it was time to leave Graham and Gillian alone.

As the honeymoon went on, however, they both felt they couldn't just cut Janet out of the picture. More and more, they insisted she joined in with them. They wanted to make sure she didn't feel awkward with them. This was her holiday as well.

So she became an essential part of the proceedings.

41

No mealtime was complete without her. The three of them would laugh and joke at all the same things. They had built up a remarkable rapport.

Graham was becoming convinced they were all having an even better time – thanks to bringing Janet along. If anything, he began to think, she was an improvement on Gillian. No, he didn't really mean that. Not *really*. It was just that she kept flitting into his thoughts – he couldn't help it. Every time he looked at Gillian, he saw Janet shining through. Maybe it was because they were so similar.

At first, he dismissed it as a natural fondness for his wife's sister. They were twins and it was obvious that he would find them both attractive. He would watch as Janet plunged into the pool for a swim. Looking at her body. Examining every minute detail – comparing it all the time to Gillian.

Janet seemed to hold herself much better. Her breasts seemed firmer. Her body seemed more shapely. But then again...

Both Graham and Gillian became quite depressed as the day of Janet's departure back to London approached. They both enjoyed her company immensely but for entirely different reasons. They didn't want to see her go. But the plane ticket was booked. It would cost a fortune to change it.

They all decided to go out for an extra special dinner the night before she was due to leave. It was like a leaving party in a way. Gillian was sad. She was going to miss her sister's company during those long, hot, sunny days on the beach.

As they sat in the corner of the restaurant, Graham proposed a toast to his sister-in-law. It was a nice gesture and Janet smiled warmly at him. He stared intently at her. Delighted that she had responded to him so openly. Gillian paused for moment. She frowned at Graham, then dismissed her suspicions as ridiculous. The dinner party continued.

Graham told a joke and the two sisters listened

carefully to his every word. After the punch line delivery, they both laughed in unison. Janet grabbed Graham's arm purely as a reaction to the wisecrack. She felt good about her brother-in-law. He seemed a fine person. Someone who would bring nothing but happiness to her family. She was pleased.

Her hand squeezed his arm gently. It was an act of fondness for a new relative she was only just beginning to get to know, but to Graham it was a significant sign. Evidence that Janet was starting to return the feelings he had for her.

If anyone else in the world had squeezed his arm in such a way, he would have thought nothing of it, but when she did it... it had to mean something. A deliberate flirtation. He couldn't accept it as anything else.

If only Janet had realised what thoughts were rushing through his mind at that moment, then maybe she would not have inadvertently brushed his leg with the toes of her shoe just a few minutes later. To her, it was an innocent movement. Not intended in any way to be interpreted as a show of affection. She didn't give it any thought at the time. She just pulled her foot away gradually so as not to appear rude.

When Graham felt the movement of her shoe on his leg, it left a completely different impression. He saw it as even more evidence of her attempt to tell him that she fancied him. That she could not wait for him to get back to England so they might make wild, passionate love.

He looked up and glanced at her as her toe rested, momentarily, on his leg. He smiled discreetly, so Gillian would not see. Janet saw the look on his face and pulled her foot away immediately – but it was already too late. The damage had been done.

Graham's obsession had begun.

The next day was a sad occasion for everyone. Graham and Gillian were both at the airport saying fond farewells to Janet. It was more like saying goodbye to a relative who was emigrating to the other side of the world, than a sister whom they would both see just seven days later.

Gillian had thought it ludicrous to take Janet to the airport. She was a grown up person, perfectly capable of looking after herself, but Graham had insisted. He told his new wife that he would expect her to do the same thing if the situations were reversed. That was just a smoke screen for the searing passion he felt for Janet. Any excuse just to spend that extra hour in her company. Just to be sitting next to her in the taxi. To feel her leg brush against his own as they got out at the other end. To smell her perfume. To see her smile. To feel her lips.

When Gillian kissed her sister fondly on the cheek before she went through passport control, Graham could feel the excitement in his stomach, anticipating the hug and kiss he knew he was about to receive. It was a rare opportunity for him to feel her in his arms. Gillian looked on, completely unaware of his innermost feelings.

When the time finally came for his turn to say good-bye, he was like a schoolboy about to experience his first kiss. He felt awkward. Almost embarrassed by the situation. After all those days and nights of fantasy, the reality was now staring him in the face.

He bent to kiss her gently on the side of her face. He wanted desperately to move his mouth over to her lips. He watched them. They were covered in just the right amount of red lipstick. He was certain that for a moment he saw them quiver with expectation but he couldn't bring himself to do more than brush the side of her cheek with his lips. He waited for a split second, breathing in her scent. Then he pulled away, once more aware of the presence of his young bride. She did not notice his reaction.

They both watched as she waved back at them while walking through customs, all the time completely unaware of the effect she had already had on their lives and the tragedy she had inadvertently set in motion.

Graham had always been an incurable romantic. But now his thoughts were working overtime. Janet consumed his waking hours. When Gillian turned to ask him a question, he ignored her – stuck in a fantasy trance. But this was no fairy tale. He was on his honeymoon, transfixed by another woman.

"Let's have a drink at the airport bar."

Graham snapped out of his daze. Gillian sensed something was wrong.

However, that request to stop for a drink had an ulterior motive. For Graham wanted to see Janet's plane as it took off for London. Like a child watching a huge airliner lift into the sky, waiting for a wave from one of those tiny round windows, Graham actually believed she might look out and see him down there.

He was already beginning to lose all sense of reality. He did not even know which side of the plane she would be sitting on. How on earth would she see him?

None of that mattered to Graham. He just wanted to feel that there might be a chance. That was enough to keep him there. Waiting for the opportunity of a glimpse.

They sat in sad silence at a table in the bar. Graham's eyes kept darting towards the runway every time an aircraft taxied for take off. Gillian did not realise how attentive he was being because he wore sunglasses.

Finally her plane appeared on the tarmac.

He watched as the jet engines thrusted it forward, faster and faster towards the end of the runway. For a split second, it seemed to falter and Graham caught his breath with fear. Surely it wouldn't crash. Please. God. No. The momentary jerk was a perfectly normal motion for the plane but Graham had feared catastrophe.

He stared through his sunglasses as it passed overhead. He felt as if someone had torn out his stomach.

He would not see her again until they returned to Orpington! He wasn't sure he could cope. The pain was so great he doubled up as if suffering from some awful bout of indigestion.

Gillian looked over, concerned that he was in agony. If she'd been able to see behind those dark glasses, she would have noticed the tears welling up in his eyes.

He managed to wipe them away before they reached his cheeks. Gillian Philpott presumed her groom was in the middle of a hay fever attack.

That night, Graham Philpott lay in bed next to his wife wide awake. She had long since fallen asleep. But he could not relax. He could not switch his mind off.

Janet. Every minute. Every second. There she was. In her bikini. Smiling in the bar. Winking at him. Embracing him, running her fingers down his chest...

His appetite had gone. He told Gillian he had a stomach bug. But he knew he'd feel hungry when he saw Janet again.

He was tense. So anxious to see his wife's twin sister. To feel her in his arms. To love her.

After hours of lying awake in the hot Bali night, Graham quietly slipped out from between the covers and crept across the room. The only noise was the constant blur of the air conditioning system and the crickets out on the balcony.

He sat down at the desk and took out some of the hotel note paper. He stared out of the window as he tried to put his thoughts in writing. After a few minutes the words started to flow.

"When I looked into your face you had such a lovely look when I was stroking your cheek."

He stopped writing for a moment. Pausing to make sure that what he had just written made sense. Then he went on.

"It was such a soft expression and I think that must have been the first time certainly that I saw that and knew certainly that I must have completely fallen in love with you."

It was a clumsy sentence but she would know what he meant.

Graham Philpott wrote for hours. He became so immersed in it, that he just gave up worrying what he would say to Gillian if she stirred from her slumber in the bed, just a few feet away.

Luckily, she slept soundly, unaware of the passionate love letter her husband was writing to her twin sister.

Janet wasn't there to meet them at the airport. That was the first disappointment. He was desperate to see her. He needed her so badly. But at least he had the letters to give to her.

Then she did not respond when he tried to call her.

Perhaps she did not want him after all. Was it possible that her loyalty to her sister over-rode her feelings for him?

Graham was worried. He did not want to give either of them up. But, if he had to, he had already decided he would choose Janet first. She was the one who would become his lover. It was only a matter of time.

Then an incident occurred that seemed to confirm all his wildest fantasies. Janet asked if she could stay on at their house. The break up of her long term relationship had had a traumatic effect on her, she explained. To Gillian, it seemed a perfectly sisterly thing to say: "Yes."

Graham could hardly contain his excitement. When she arrived at the front door, he took all her bags upstairs to the spare bedroom and layed them all out lovingly on the duvet.

Janet was surprised. Men normally didn't bother. But she gave it little thought.

Those slightly wary feelings she had about Graham in Bali were long since gone. She was just grateful to have a place to stay. She did not really think he had a serious crush on her. Gillian, on the other hand, noticed that things seemed well... different.

A few weeks later they accepted an invitation to a neighbours' party. It was a rare treat for the twins. Graham was not a great spender and the chance to dress up came but once or twice a month. As Janet came down the stairs wearing a pretty red dress, Graham looked up from the hallway.

"Janet. You look marvellous. What a beautiful dress. You really know how to look good don't you?"

His smile seemed never ending. He could not stop looking at her body. Admiring every aspect of it as she gave them both the customary twirl.

As Graham poured compliment after compliment out, Gillian stood beside him in the room. He had not said one word about her outfit. She felt upset by his neglect. But she put it down to thoughtlessness.

Parties in Orpington tended to be pretty staid affairs. When Gillian, Graham and Janet turned up at their neighbour's semi-detached home, they were a breath of fresh air compared to the grey-looking people at the gathering.

Smartly, but sexily dressed, the two sisters prompted a number of glances from the mainly middle-aged men assembled. Graham was lapping up the attention. In his mind, he had not one, but two of the prettiest girls in the street on his arm.

More people began to arrive and the party picked up. Then the hosts turned up the music. The sixties sounds brought a lot of memories back for Graham. He watched as some of the couples danced in the front room. The effect of the alcohol had loosened their suburban outlook and some people were actually enjoying themselves. Gillian wandered off to talk to a friend. It left Graham on his own with Janet. For a moment, there was a difficult silence between them. He was lost for words. His love for her was so over-whelming that he didn't know what to say. Anything would have sounded ridiculous. He could hardly blurt out "I love you" in front of a crowded party.

Janet construed his silence as shyness. She decided

to break the ice.

"Why don't we dance?"

It was an innocent enough request, but to a man as besotted as he was, it sounded like an gift from god. A confirmation of his delusion.

It was not as if they were even about to dance closely together. Janet would never have even considered that option. She simply intended to bop around to the music for a few minutes. Nothing more. She now knew he had a crush on her. It was obvious. She just hoped it would go away.

As they danced, Graham watched and soaked up the way she moved. From the twisting of her hips to the movement of her thighs, he could not take his eyes off her. Like a lot of men when they dance, he was barely moving. She had no idea he was examining her every move. Lusting after her. Imagining she was making love to him. But when she saw his eyes, they were a dead give away. They were boring deep into hers. She thought it was probably the effect of the drink. But it made her feel uncomfortable. She did not like being stared at so intently by any man – certainly not her brother-in-law.

To Graham there was no going back.

When a person is obsessed they lose sight of reality. They believe that every sign is significant. Every movement becomes yet more proof of affection.

Later, he tape recorded a message to her – referring to that fateful first dance.

"It was the first time I really had an opportunity of dancing with you the way I really wanted to. God, I can feel it now. I think it is probably the best way I have ever danced. I was moving to the way your body was moving and I was certainly responding the way you were. If anyone was watching my eyes they must have known I was so in love with you."

To Gillian Philpott, the signs were also becoming all too apparent. She had played the good samaritan and allowed her sister to stay at their home. Now she was abusing that hospitality by having what appeared to be a love affair with her husband. Gillian just could not believe the relationship was only one-way. It took two, that was her attitude. And now she was building up a hatred for them both.

It was December, 1989, and after just one year of married life, Gillian wished she had never agreed to the wedding. Everything was going wrong for them.

The marriage had just been a piece of paper, a confirmation of what they already knew. But now it seemed to have sealed their fate. She felt the relationship crumbling the moment they had returned from the honeymoon. He no longer listened to anything she said. Instead, he heaped praise on Janet constantly while barely acknowledging her existance.

Gillian would walk into rooms where they both were and become immediately struck by the overwhelming silence – as if they had been talking secretly until the moment she entered. At meal times, Graham would respond so lovingly to Janet's conversation. Always looking deep into her eyes whenever they spoke. Gillian would just sit there. Neglected. Unwanted.

In bed at night it was just the same story. He wasn't interested any more. Gillian came to the same conclusion millions of wives the world over do every day. She decided he must be seeing another woman – and it could only be Janet.

But, so far, she had no firm evidence. She had never caught them actually kissing. Not even touching and certainly nothing sexual. The torture of not knowing for sure was, in some ways, even worse than knowing for certain. At least then she could get on with her life and find another man. Start afresh. She was only 27. Easily young enough to meet and marry someone new. Someone who would make her happy. But, without any evidence, it was difficult to confront them.

Once, she cornered Janet on her own, while Graham

was outside washing the car.

"Are you having an affair with him? Just tell me the truth."

Janet was astounded. She had no idea what her sister was thinking. As far as she was concerned, Graham had a silly crush. She would not have even entertained the thought of having an affair with him. As far as Janet was concerned, she had never once encouraged Graham. It was all in his head.

She assured her sister there was "no truth in it whatsoever". But she knew that the atmosphere in that house could only get worse.

Gillian kept watching, waiting for the signs.

She became convinced her sister was lying. How could he get that infatuated with her unless she was returning his affections?

Gillian could not get the relationship out of her mind.

Janet and Graham had just gone out Christmas shopping together. That would give them all sorts of opportunities for a liaison. A chance to express their love for one another. He could even be assuring her that he would leave his wife.

All these thoughts were rushing through Gillian's mind as she sat alone at the house one afternoon. She had to know one way or another. The anguish could not go on much longer. There had to be a way to find out for certain.

She went upstairs to Janet's bedroom, determined to discover the truth. She felt no guilt as she systematically rifled through her twin sister's bags. There had to be some evidence. Some shred of proof that they were having an affair. Underneath a pile of clothing in one case, she found an envelope. Inside it was a card. Something within her cried This is it.

On the cover, it looked like a perfectly normal Christmas card. But inside, the message was loud and clear "To my darling, I wish you every happiness at Christmas. I am so fortunate to spend my life with

51

you always."

Gillian began to cry. Now she had found out the truth, it really hurt. Maybe she should never have gone snooping for it in the first place.

Then she could have carried on in the hope they could mend their marriage. Now she was faced with the facts. But she had wanted to know. She had to find out.

The tears streamed down her face. The feeling of betrayal. The disappointment. But she had to get a hold of herself. She had to confront them. This was it. This was all the evidence Gillian required.

She went back downstairs and waited. She knew they had to come back from that shopping trip eventually. Then she would destroy them. She would tell them what she thought of them.

She first heard them approach as they walked up the short driveway to the house. Janet was laughing. Graham was telling her a joke and she was responding warmly. Gillian watched through the net curtains that hid so many secrets in the suburban world she lived in. It incensed her to see them so happy together.

As she heard the key being turned in the front door lock, she braced herself for her onslaught. This time they could not deny it. There was no way they could claim this Christmas card was anything other than a token of their love for one another.

Janet and Graham looked up and smiled as Gillian approached them in the hallway. But, within moments, they could tell that something was wrong. Gillian looked flushed with fury. The tears had long gone. Their place had been taken by seething anger. The time had come.

"She's got to go."

Janet was stunned to hear what her twin sister – her own flesh and blood – was saying.

Graham was not so surprised. He knew it would come to this one day. He wanted it to reach a head, so that Gillian could no longer control it.

"Then you will have to go as well."

Graham's voice was cool, collected. The words spoken almost silkily, but with menace underneath.

The tables had turned. Gillian – the one who had just discovered her sister was having what she thought was an affair with her husband – was now being made to feel like the villain.

For a few moments these three relatives looked at one another.

But the anger that had been building up inside Gillian had turned to fear. Fear that she was about to lose her home and her husband. Underneath it all, she hoped that by confronting them both she could drive Janet out of the house and then they could start afresh.

But now her world had been turned upside down. She was confused. She knew that deep inside, she still loved Graham – no matter what he had or had not done with her twin sister.

"Please love me." She begged. "Not her."

Gillian was feeling desperate now. Her sister had run upstairs to pack her things leaving the couple alone to face each other.

"Have all the affairs you want, if I don't satisfy you. But you'll never find another woman who would do all the things I did for you."

Gillian was getting hysterical. She was straining her face to avoid crying.

"I'll do anything you want to make our marriage work. You must believe me. I love you so much."

Graham Philpott did not react to her pleas. Instead, he said coldly, "I want a divorce from you."

Gillian was allowed to continue sleeping in the house – but only in the spare bedroom where her sister Janet had once slept. To all the neighbours in Mungo Park Way, who wished them "Happy Christmas" when they passed in the street, Graham and Gillian Philpott seemed as close as ever that December. They went to a stream of parties in the area as man and wife – never once revealing the anguish of their break up.

Janet had left the house on the day of their big confrontation, never to return. She was as bemused as she was hurt by the whole episode. Graham flooded her life with cards and messages. His obsessive love had not in any way been dampened by those scenes at the house. Instead, he thought about how they would be together one day. He sent her a loving note saying, "Thank you for giving me a lovely year. It is so lovely living with you."

It was signed: "From your loving Graham."

Now, Gillian and Graham were keeping up a huge pretence to the outside world. Deceiving everyone into believing they were as happy as ever.

Christmas Day was a disaster. They barely spoke to one another. It was supposed to be a time of year for rejoicing. For Gillian and Graham it was a time for silence.

The only respite for both of them were the parties they attended in the neighbourhood. These seemed to provide them with an escape from the appalling situation at home. As soon as they arrived at any party, they would split up and head off for conversations with people on opposite sides of the room. It was a bizarre existence. No communication at home but a smiling veneer at every public function.

By the time New Year 1990 was almost upon them, the strain was really starting to tell.

On December 30, Gillian and Graham managed just enough conversation between themselves to agree to go to a neighbour for a drinks party. As usual, within seconds of arriving, they split up and headed in different directions.

But, as other guests were later to remark, they still made a point of making it absolutely clear just how much in love they still were. In one extraordinary conversation, Graham told a friend, "We are thinking of going to Bali for a second honeymoon." Perhaps he

54

was thinking of Janet at the time? It was an astonishing remark to make when one considered the circumstances.

Gillian may have hated him for his obsession, but she still longed to live the rest of her life with him. She still wanted him to love her. To adore her. To want her. Even though they had not even slept in the same bed for weeks she lived in hope.

But the pressure of the situation was leading them both to drink excessively.

And at that neighbour's party, they both went over the top...

It was two-thirty a.m. by the time they stumbled into their house.

Graham was looking for an argument.

"I just don't care for you any more," he said. "We must get a divorce."

They were standing in the hall. He was not giving her a single ounce of compassion.

Gillian longed for him. She really wanted to sleep with him that night. Feel his body next to hers. Feel the warmth and security they had enjoyed together for so many years.

"Can I come to bed with you. Please."

He did not reply.

"Please let me sleep there tonight. I won't go near you. I won't touch you if that's what you want."

But Graham's thoughts were only for Janet – even then.

"I don't want you. Can't you understand that?"

He was shouting fiercely now.

"I don't want you." He kept repeating it over and over.

Even then Gillian felt a compulsion to try to please him in any way she thought might bring him back to her.

"I'll bring Janet back into the house. Anything."

"You're a bitch. You should never have thrown Janet out."

Gillian still kept pleading.

"But surely this isn't worth giving up eight years of happiness for?"

She was trying to appeal to his good sense now. The sensible side of him that made him such a right and proper person for his job. But he only wanted one thing now – the divorce settlement.

"I've lost a house and money before. But this time, you're entitled to nothing."

That was the final straw for Gillian. He had switched this screaming match from the subject of love to money. In her mind, it showed just what he really thought of her. It proved that he was a cold, calculating man. Not the loving person she once knew so well.

He was shouting more at her now. He kept on and on about the money. She took the pink dressing gown cord from around her waist and gripped it tightly in her fist – just in case.

He was losing control. Everything he said was becoming increasingly hurtful. Then, as he swayed around in the room, he grabbed Gillian by the neck. She did not know if it was because he was falling or trying to throttle her. But she grasped the dressing gown cord in both hands and twisted it around his neck. He felt his throat tightening as the cord dug into his windpipe. Nothing would stop her now. There was no marriage to look forward to – he had seen to that. Gillian Philpott felt the urge to pull that cord tighter and tighter. She could see his eyes bulging outwards as he tried to free himself. But the surprise element had given Gillian just a few moments in which to seal his fate. He had already begun to die. He simply did not have the energy left to fight back.

She gave the cord one more sharp pull and her husband was dead.

It had all been so quick and, in a strange way, so painless.

For a few seconds she sat there stunned by her own actions. What had she done? It was awful as the feeling began to dawn on her. She had just killed Graham –

the man she once loved so dearly. The man who had given her the happiest days of her life.

But he had taken his own life. He had demanded death and been given it in the end.

Gillian looked at his twisted body on the floor and knew she had to do something to make him look as if he'd committed suicide. She wanted to die with him.

Using all her strength, she picked up his lifeless body by putting her arms under his and pulling hard. She stopped by the bannisters at the landing and tied a fresh, longer piece of cord around his neck.

Then she knotted the other end firmly to a bannister.

It was no easy task to lift his 12 stone body over the edge of the rail. For minutes she struggled until, through sheer will power she managed to tip it over the edge.

Exhausted, she sat down on the bed for a few minutes, trying to compose herself so she could plan the next stage. She thought about Graham. What he meant to her. What, ultimately, she had ended up meaning to him. That gave her the strength to carry on. She got out a sheet of their headed notepaper and paused for a few seconds to decide what to write. It was not that difficult.

"We couldn't live separately. We wanted to die together. Please keep us together – I beg of you. We love one another so much."

And she meant every word.

Gillian Philpott grabbed at the bottle of aspirins in the medicine cupboard. She was going to do it. She was going to kill herself. End it all. There was nothing left to live for.

She had lived through the worst nightmare of all and now it was time to say goodbye. To leave this world and all her problems behind. The note was written. Now she had to go through with it.

She struggled with the childproof cap of the aspirin bottle for what seemed like minutes, in a desperate effort to get at the tablets. Finally she managed to pull off the lid and put the bottle to her lips. The bitter tasting pills cascaded smoothly into her mouth. She stopped and took a huge swig from the bottle of whisky that stood on the table besides her. Soon she had finished off the bottle of about 30 pills and sat down to die.

She presumed that the tightness in her stomach was a sign that the tablets were getting into her bloodstream. Poisoning her permanently. She hoped it would be quick. Suddenly, a terrible nauseous feeling overwhelmed her. Her stomach began to spasm. Uncontrolable jerking movements. She could feel the bitter taste of the pills against the roof of her mouth. She vommited everywhere. A steady stream gushed out of her like an oil well.

She would have to try something else. The determination to end it all was still there.

It was early morning on December 31, 1990. Gillian Philpott was trying to concentrate on the road as she drove the couple's Ford Orion on the busy 'A' road full of New Year's Eve traffic.

Just a few hours earlier, she had killed the husband she had always loved so much and then tried to kill herself. Unsuccessfully. Now she intended to finish off the job in such a way there would be no room for failure.

As she approached the cliffs of Beachy Head – a picturesque beauty spot on the Sussex coast renowned for suicide bids – she kept rehearsing her death plunge plans.

She wanted to make sure there was no mistake this time. She wanted to join Graham in heaven. At least Janet was not there.

There were quite a number of sightseers at Beachy Head that day watching hang gliders sweep majestically up into the skies from the cliff edge, hundreds of feet above sea level.

Gillian clutched onto the steering wheel as the car mounted the grass verge that led to the cliff edge. Her foot flat down on the accelerator, she willed the car forward as fast as it would go. This was the worst part. The waiting. The waiting to die.

She felt the car rear forward as the engine over-revved. Getting closer and closer to that leap into the unknown.

No-one was watching the Ford. All eyes were on the hang gliders soaring on the thermals.

Gillian felt a weird sensation as the car got near the edge. It was a mixture of elation and fear. She was relieved it would soon all be over. But she was terrified of the pain she might have to endure before the moment of death.

Then it happened. The car lifted over the edge of the precipice. She was flying through the air. Totally out of control now. Completely unable to stop fate from taking a hand.

She felt her head hit the steering wheel as the car smacked the ground. Then everything went dark.

"There's a car in the bushes."

The voice of the hang glider pilot was most emphatic.

Amateur photographer David Payne reacted immediately by rushing over to the place where the pilot had pointed.

Two policemen followed just seconds later and scrambled down to the Ford Orion. Gillian had been sick and was naturally distressed. But there was no lasting damage. Incredibly, she only sustained minor injuries after smashing her head on the steering wheel. The car had dropped only twenty feet onto a ledge that jutted out of the cliff.

It did not take long for forensic scientists to conclude that Graham Philpot had been murdered.

At the Old Bailey, in January, 1991, Gillian Philpott was found guilty of the manslaughter of her husband and sentenced to just two years imprisonment. Her sister Janet always emphatically denied having any sexual relations with Graham Philpott.

3

The Black Widow

Winnacunnet High School was the sort of place educationalists dream about.

Nestling on the edge of the quiet New England town of Hampton, it enjoyed a reputation as one of the finest schools in the North Eastern United States. None of those classic inner city problems of violence and truancy existed here. This was middle America. Simple. No Frills. A pleasant environment where people were at peace with themselves.

The white wood detached houses with their neatly trimmed front lawns that dominated the area, were classic evidence of that harmony. The immaculately clean streets throughout the picture postcard town centre summed up the pride which residents of Hampton had in their town. It was a relatively small, tightly knit community where everyone knew each other. There was a familiarity about the place that made you feel instantly at home.

All in all it represented a fairly large chunk of the American dream. Virtually no crime and even fewer scandals.

And the sons and daughters of Hampton residents were brought up to honour and obey those rules. While many of them were allowed their own car by the age of sixteen, there was a strictly enforced alcohol rule that prevented any person under the age of thirty from buying booze unless they provided an ID card.

Parents were determined to bring their children up in a responsible way. Constantly lecturing them about the evils of drink and drugs. Always preventing them from doing anything wild.

It was the same in the classrooms of Winnacunnet High. That strict moral code was abided by to the letter. And anyone who stepped out of line was severeley punished. But, out of all this discipline, there were, inevitably, the rebels. The youngsters who only wanted to do the opposite of what their family hoped for. The teenagers who saw that all these rules and regulations were made to be broken.

Bill Flynn, Patrick Randall and Vance Lattime were weary of being repressed by their parents. They were sick and tired of conforming. They wanted to be different.

As the three 15-year-olds hung around in the school playground one cold November day, discussing how awful their families were, there seemed to be little in life for them to look forward to. College exams were fast approaching and they were under constant pressure to perform well. To them, learning was not an interesting pastime. It was that common bond of apathy that sealed their friendship. They had all recognised in each other a total disdain for schoolwork. It drew them together.

Each time one of them was in trouble in class, it became a very special mark of distinction. The other two would look on proudly when their friend was punished. They saw it as yet more evidence of why they had to get out of school as quickly as possible – which was quite a problem for the three friends.

The staff at Winnacunnet pushed relentlessly for their pupils to go on to college – no matter what. Academically and sportingly, they were all expected to excel. But Bill, Patrick and Vance had other ideas. In an attempt to separate themselves from the majority of hard working classmates, they even decided to call themselves "The Three Musketeers".

"That way people will know we are different," said Bill. He had become the self-appointed ring leader despite looking even younger than his years.

Basically, Bill, Patrick and Vance were more intrigued by the girls in their grade than the history of art. Their idea of fun was discussing the prowess of their favourite girls – even though they might never have even touched them.

"Hey. Wouldn't you just love to...." Bill was trying to get a response out of his quieter friend Vance. They were discussing what they would like to do to one particularly sexy looking blonde classmate. She was glancing over in their direction from the other side of the playground. She seemed to be encouraging them. Maybe she could hear what they were saying?

The boys were smirking. Excited at the prospect. They had interpreted the girl's acknowledgement as a certain invitation for sex – even though none of them had uttered more than a few words to her. In truth, she was just flirting in that inimitable way only teenage girls can. Just glancing every so often. Encouraging the boys' adolescent minds at every moment.

The Three Musketeers had another good reason to get out of school at the earliest opportunity. They were all virgins. But they didn't like admitting it to themselves – let alone their pals. They tended to swap imaginary tales of their sexual conquests in the hope it would convince their pals what experienced men they really were.

"Maybe she's just after your body Vance," said Bill when he spotted Vance staring wistfully in the direction of that pretty classmate.

From the opposite corner of the playground, another older woman was watching the three boys. But they did not notice.

Class was about to restart – and that meant more mindless learning.

They quickly shared a cigarette butt in the corner of the vast grey concrete covered playground and all agreed there must be more to life than just school. They were all about to find out. A lot sooner than they realised.

The older woman was still watching the threesome. Holding back. She was waiting for the perfect moment to make her approach. When the bell rang, the Three Musketeers hastily stubbed out their sneaky cigarette and sloped off towards the double doors that led to the main school corridor.

"Hello Billy," teacher Pamela Smart had just caught up with the boy.

Bill was slightly embarrassed in front of his pals. It was all very well talking about women, but it wasn't so easy when they confronted you head on.

He had met Pamela Smart for the first time the previous evening when she ran a self-esteem class for teenagers from the school. She seemed so mature and adult to Bill – even though there was only five years between them. He had found himself glancing incessantly at her legs as she leaned against the teacher's desk in that classroom the night before. She had good legs for a teacher. Even a pretty face with a fashionable streaked blonde hairstyle.

He had tried to make out her breasts beneath her loose fitting knitted jumper, and when he lay in bed that night, Billy thought about those brief glimpses of her upper thighs. It might not have been reality but then he knew, from her wedding ring, that she would never become anything more than a figure to put in that memory bank, which can provide the perfect fantasy on demand.

Now, here she was approaching him in the playground.

"Will you please come to my office after school Billy. It's important," she said almost coldly. Pamela Smart then walked off in the opposite direction.

The other two Musketeers were sniggering.

"Hey. Billy baby. Maybe it'll be your lucky night!"

They were amused by the use of the name 'Billy', as opposed to the macho 'Bill'. But that adolescent theory on why she wanted to see Bill seemed a far fetched notion at the time. His thoughts were completely opposite to those of his friends. He was furious that he was going to have to stay on at school. He never liked to spend a moment longer than was absolutely necessary inside those four grey walls.

But he was puzzled all the same. She had offered no explanation. Just a direct order. It was as if she didn't want to hear any reply. He just had to obey. It was as simple as that.

Pamela's office at Winnacunnet High School was hardly a grand affair. Surrounded with shelves crammed with schoolbooks, it consisted of a table and two chairs – just enough space for her to type undisturbed.

As media studies teacher at the school, she was afforded the luxury of her own office, because she had other duties besides teaching. They included the onorous task of writing and then distributing press releases to the local newspaper and television stations about certain school events.

It was a relentless battle. And there were times when Pamela really wondered why she bothered. So little of her material was ever acted upon. She had landed the teaching job thanks to her own virtually obsessive knowledge of the media. And this was one of the drawbacks.

It was her work as a DJ on a local heavy rock station, that had sparked off her interest. She regularly indulged herself by playing her own special brand of really loud, raucous music to an audience of listeners who really appreciated her efforts. It was a part-time, unpaid job. But just to get the chance to play her favourite band Van Halen over and and over again was reward in itself. It was her way of turning the clock back to her teenage years. Something she seemed to be doing more and more.

The staff at the radio station particularly enjoyed Pam's visits, because she always went to great effort to wear really sexy clothes – like skin tight jeans and lots of leather.

Pam loved the heavy thudding bass lines and the screaming vocals. Heavy metal music made her feel really good if she was down. She idolised Van Halen in every way possible. She would have done anything to meet them in person.

Pam also had a softer, more charitable side to her nature in sharp contrast to her passion for those brutal heavy metal sounds. She used to be happy to help out at the school by teaching to the school's self-esteem programme for teenagers. After all, she herself had only just come out of her teens and she knew just what it was like. She got a real buzz out of helping the kids to discover themselves. It was a vital part of the growing up process as far as she was concerned.

The past few months had been a time of great upheaval for Pam. The previous May she had married her college sweetheart, Greg. They had moved into a comfortable apartment in nearby Derry, New Hampshire. But, as a salesman, he was often away and she found it difficult being on her own at home so often, with only the dog for company. That was another reason why she had volunteered to teach the programme.

In the class that previous evening, she had clearly noticed Bill Flynn studying her body. She did not think Bill noticed the wry smile that came to her lips at that moment. Maybe it was just as well.

It was hardly a new experience for Pam. As a young female teacher, a lot of the boy pupils would lust after her. Imagining what they would like to do to her. Stripping her with their eyes. Fantasising about bedroom encounters.

It amused her. When she was a pupil at school herself, she had always been the girl who would flirt in the playground. She used to love teasing them by leaving a button undone or pursing her lips. It was fun. So good for one's confidence. She missed the attention she used to get from all those boys. It just wasn't the same once you had grown up. People expected you to behave more responsibly. You could no longer act wild.

Pam would often flashback to those days when she found herself jealously watching the kids in the playground at Winnacunnet doing exactly the same thing. She wished she could do it all over again.

When Pam spotted Billy in the playground that morning, she felt compelled to do something. He was such a nice looking boy with that mane of dark wavey hair and those sea blue eyes. She had watched as he and his friends flirted with that blonde schoolgirl on the other side of the playground. She wanted Bill to notice her and flirt with her – but he didn't.

Now she had him all to herself here in her office.

"Sit down Billy," said Pamela, as the teenager stepped nervously into the room.

Bill was still puzzled. He could not quite work out why Pamela had made him stay late. Maybe she had noticed him leering at her the previous evening and wanted to reprimand him? If that was the case, he felt highly embarrassed. It was all very well thinking those dirty thoughts but he didn't want to be confronted with them by the object of his fantasies.

Few words passed between them before she produced an envelope and gave it to him. He did not question why. But just opened it.

"I hope you like them," was all she said.

It was clear from the package they were family snap shots. Perhaps she was trying to relax him by showing him pictures of her family before she punished him. Bill was very confused. What on earth was she handing them to me for? he wondered.

"Go on. Go ahead and look," insisted Pamela.

Before opening the package, Bill hesitated for a moment. None of this made any sense. It was ridiculous.

He was about to ask why when Pam repeated "Go on. Open it." He felt compelled to do as he was told. As he took the snapshots out of the packet, he froze. His eyes were feasting upon the photograph on top of the pile. Bill was speechless. Stunned by the contents. He could not believe what was happening.

Picture after picture showed Pamela in just the way he had dreamt about her the previous evening. But she had an even better figure. He did not realise teachers could have such fantastic bodies.

She was wearing the briefest of bikinis in every shot. But it was the look on her face that said it all, loud and clear. She had a sensual gleam in her eyes. They said: "Come here. I want you." For a moment, he wondered if these were taken just before she had sex. All the evidence seemed to point to that conclusion.

Her body was far more sensational than it could ever seem in the classroom. His pals would not believe him if he told them.

Bill was having trouble keeping his hands from shaking. He was still bewildered. Here he was sitting in a teacher's office at school while she showed him the sexiest set of pictures he had ever seen in his life. They might not have been as graphic as the soft porn mag he had flicked through at a friend's house only a few days previously, but this was a real person – not some dolly girl whose name in the captions probably did not even exist. The model in this case was sitting opposite him in that very room.

Pam was watching his reaction with interest. She could see him fidgeting uncomfortably in his seat. She wanted him to relax. She knew she was going to have to lead the way. She wondered if he really was a virgin after all. Somehow, she thought, he was.

She stood up and walked around to the side of the desk where Bill was sitting. He looked at her in a daze, unable to cope with what was happening. The photos still clutched in his clamy hands.

She knew he was bewildered. It was exactly how she wanted him. She wanted to be the dominating force. Leading the way with every move. Only deciding what *she* wanted to do. He just had to obey her.

Then she leant against the desk in exactly the same way she had done on the previous night. It was a deliberately provocative act. She wanted an excuse. She needed to have that control over him.

She kept repeating the lines to her favourite Van

Halen song *Hot For Teacher*. It was all about the seduction of a pupil by his teacher.

Pam wriggled her hips ever so slightly to losen up the tight fitting skirt she was wearing. Bill was at last beginning to realise that his teacher had seen every one of his reactions the previous evening. She had obviously enjoyed every glance. Now he had an extraordinary opportunity to translate those fantasies into reality.

Pam stroked his hair gently. Touching and probing with one hand. The other traced circles around the inside of his ear lobe. Then she picked up the photos and handed them to Bill. "Find the one you like best."

To Bill, every picture was too hot to handle. They were all as suggestive as each other. He wasn't interested in the pictures. He wanted the real thing.

"You've got to pick out the best one Bill," she repeated her request. But, by now, it had become an order. Bill showed her a shot of her on all fours taken from behind. It was an incredibly provocative photograph.

On the day she posed, Pam had been determined to act as sexily as possible – twisting her body in a way that would maximise her ultimate message to whoever she showed them to. As her best friend Tracey Collins took the photos, she kept repeating: "Do you think they are sexy enough. Tell me they are. Tell me they are."

She hoped it would turn on her husband Greg. But, instead, he was appalled and demanded that she destroy the pictures. He craved respectability not all this sordidness.

"Well if he doesn't like the pictures I'll find someone else who will," she thought to herself.

Now she was about to put those pictures to the test by using them to seduce a 15-year-old boy.

Bill sat there in her office, still drifting in and out of reality. At one point he decided it must all be a dream. His mind began to wander. Then he felt

Pamela's hand stroking and caressing. It was all becoming very real once more.

Suddenly, Pamela pulled her hand away from Bill's lap. She had heard voices outside the door to her office. Bill came to. Snapped out of his sexual trance. Perhaps taking a split second longer to register the disturbance nearby.

"Don't worry Billy. You'll have me next time," she whispered.

Next day found Billy wandering around the playground in a trance of disbelief. Had she really shown him those photos? His fellow musketeers were worried. "What's wrong Bill? You ill or something?" Vance said.

Bill's mind was elsewhere.

He could not stop thinking about her. The chance to break his virginity had been so close and yet so far last night. But at least he now had a chance to actually lose it with a real woman – not some giggling classmate with as little experience as him.

The strange aspect was that Bill also felt a great deal of affection for Pamela. He didn't see her as a grand seducer only interested in satisfying her own sexual desires. Rather, he portrayed her as a beautiful woman who actually wanted him for more than just his young, lithe body.

It was for that reason Bill decided to break his code of friendship within the Three Musketeers and not tell them about his encounter with her – for the time being at least. If she ever found out that he'd been blabbing he'd lose his chance for good.

Across the other side of the playground, Pamela was watching and waiting once more. This time Bill noticed her instantly. That delighted her. She wanted that attention – and now she was getting it.

Minutes later, in the corridor, she touched his arm gently and said: "Come to my home tonight." She passed him a scrap of paper with her address. The appointment was set. It was now only a matter of time.

69

Bill was ecstatic.

Pamela had been planning this moment in her mind for a long time. She was fed up with those lonely nights in front of the TV screen with only her mongrel dog for company. She had kept asking Greg to change jobs so he could be around more. But, as he continually explained to her, it was not that easy. She was resigned to spending at least half the nights of the year alone. Once a week, she would host the heavy rock radio show. That was real fun. She adored the music and people at the station. They all seemed to have a much better life than her.

But the rest of her life seemed painfully empty.

When she had first met Greg at that teenage party, all those years ago, he had seemed just like her. With his shoulder length hair and love of heavy metal music they seemed to have so much in common. Both loved nights out with their mutual friends.

Greg looked like Jon Bon Jovi, and behaved like him sometimes. She liked that badness in him then. It was such a happy time for Pamela. She used to love dressing up in her heavy metal studded leather jackets and skirts, often adding fishnet stockings – oozing sex to all around her but still retaining a one-woman one-man passion for Greg. At rock concerts around the entire country, they and their friends would head bang to the hypnotic sounds, like millions of other teenagers.

Then Greg took a job as an insurance salesman and cut off all his long locks. He wanted to turn the clock forward and grow up. Pamela wanted to stay young and carefree.

Calling herself the Maiden of Metal, she took on the part-time job at the radio station and kept playing her Van Halen tracks. She began to think more and more about their message. They would always be her inspiration.

While Greg was settling down, with a safe career and a nice home, she was still firmly anchored in a teenage world of heavy metal, wild friends and all night parties.

Only a few weeks earlier, they had had an awful row when Greg announced he was going ski-ing with some friends. Pam was furious. How could he leave her alone after all those nights he had been away for work? They really screamed at each other that night. She even told Greg she wished they'd never got married.

"You've just become some boring yuppie. You're not the man I married."

To Greg, it was a painful insult. He retaliated in a crushing outburst and poured out the details of a sordid one night stand he had had some weeks earlier.

Pam was horrified. She felt betrayed. But that feeling turned to anger when he explained: "I was really drunk at the time. I didn't know what I was doing."

In her eyes, that was no excuse. From that day on her hated for him grew like a cancer, gnawing away at her insides.

Now she waited for her 15-year-old virgin pupil to arrive so she could give him her lessons in love. Just the mere thought of what she would do to Bill excited her as she waited there in the modest two-bedroomed apartment.

She had planned it all with great precision. Greg had hurt her. Now she was intending to get her revenge. Earlier that evening, she went to the video store to rent *Nine and a Half Weeks*. Pamela had seen it once before with husband Greg. They had both found it a real turn on. Now she was hoping it would have the same effect on Bill. Even the fridge was filled with beers to guarantee that the teenager would feel completely in the mood.

The stage was set. It just needed the other player.

The other player was feeling very nervous. The air of expectancy that he had felt earlier had now dissolved into a very real masculine fear that he might not be able to perform. After all, he had never had sex before in his young life. What happened if he climaxed too soon? How would he know what parts of her body were the most sensitive? He knew she would have to lead him and educate him.

As he rang the door bell something inside him half wished she wouldn't be there. Then he could just turn round and walk home. Escape the embarrassment of not being experienced. He genuinely feared that she thought he had slept with at least three or four women already.

But Pam was only too well aware of his limitations. It pleased her to think that she was going to teach him so much. It made her feel wonderful that she could influence every aspect of their relationship. She had complete power over him. Perhaps even enough power to persuade him to carry out the ultimate sacrifice?

As she opened her front door she felt a surge of excitement rushing through her body. She knew he was hungry to learn – and she wanted so badly to be his teacher. Bill also felt an instant rush of adrenaline. But it was for a different reason from her. In those few moments it took her to open the door, his attitude had undergone a complete about-turn. His guilt had evaporated. He was now desperate to have her. This was going to be it. All those fears about sex had been stupid. Now he just wanted it. Wanted it really badly.

Pam's medium length hair was no longer tied back. Instead she had it falling neatly around her face. The make-up was more elaborate than at school. Her lips were glossed. They had seemed thin before. Now they were much fuller. Enveloping. Coaxing. She licked her top lip. Her tight fitting skirt was much further above the knee than any skirt she had worn to school. She was wearing flesh coloured tights, or were they stockings? He was desperate to find out. He could see just a hint of her bust and a bra through the opened top three buttons of her blouse.

Pam and Bill were not even inside the apartment yet. But the atmosphere was clearly sexually charged.

That much was patently obvious to Pamela's friend Cecilia Pierce. She was sitting on the settee in the lounge when the couple walked in from the hallway.

Bill was taken aback. He had not expected to see Cecilia here. Perhaps he'd got it all wrong? Maybe Pam's behaviour the previous night was just a tease? How could she invite a friend along when she was planning the great seduction. It just did not make sense.

A look of obvious disappointment came over Bill's face. Both women could see it clearly.

"Hey. Billy," said Pam. "I got a really hot movie for us all to watch."

But Billy wasn't listening. His mind was racing ahead. Either he had imagined the incident in the office or perhaps he was going to end up with both these women tonight? What an experience that would be, he thought.

Soon, all three were sitting back, transfixed by the video of *Nine And A Half Weeks*.

Basinger's character Elizabeth begins the film by rejecting sex-mad Rourke, saying: "You're taking a hell of a lot for granted."

In Pam's sitting room that evening, Bill was just praying he could.

But, back on celluloid, it wasn't long before Rourke got his woman in a sex scene that is said to have been one of the steamiest in Hollywood history.

Bill watched open mouthed as Rourke's character "John" blindfolded "Elizabeth". Perhaps that's what Pam wanted to do to him?

The atmosphere in the sitting room was expectant, to say the least. All three were transfixed as "John" took an ice cube out of a glass of whisky and began dripping drops of ice cold water onto Elizabeth's body. Then he rubbed the cube over her lips before sensuously stroking the beautiful actress's nipples. Finally, he traced the edge of her panties with an ice cube between his teeth.

It was an outrageous scene, deliberately scripted to give maximum titilation to the audience. It was certainly having the desired effect on the three watching.

Pam was already planning precisely how she would make Bill re-enact the film in her bedroom. As Kim Basinger performed a really hot striptease as part of yet another seduction scene with Mickey Rourke, Bill hoped Pam would do the same for him later on. At one stage, Kim become Pam as his imagination began to work overtime.

They they watched spellbound as Mickey Rourke ravaged Kim Basinger up against a wall in a street. Torrents of water cascaded over the two stars as they tried at least six different positions.

"Wow. He's got a great body," both the girls were giggling in schoolgirl fashion as the camera followed the contours of Rourke's body.

Bill looked away embarrassed for a moment by the naked male form. But soon his eyes were once more glued to the TV set, as Basinger's figure was exploited to the full.

It was clearly one of Pam's favourite movies. She fidgeted and crossed, then uncrossed, her legs throughout. Her tight skirt rode higher and higher up her thighs. She knew it was happening but she did not care. She could feel the rush of cool air going between her legs.

Bill knew that if he had to stand up it would be embarrassing because of his huge erection. He looked over toward Pam. He could clearly see her stocking tops and the contrasting bare flesh above. At that moment, they watched Basinger – dressed in black stockings and figure hugging pencil skirt – masturbating while she fantasised over Rourke.

Earlier that day, Pamela had informed Cecilia she was inviting the youngster round, telling her in no uncertain terms that she wanted to have the boy. But she wanted Cecilia to pretend to be his girlfriend if anyone called round unexpectedly. The irony was that Cecilia was nearer to his age – she was just 16. But she realised that Pam needed to have her around as

74

cover in case Greg got back from a ski-ing trip early. It certainly would not do if he walked in on Pam and Bill alone. Greg was a jealous man.

"It must be giving you a few ideas Bill." The movie was almost over but the real action was only just beginning as far as Pam was concerned.

On the screen, Basinger was walking away from Rourke, having rejected one of his perverse requests for the last time. She had decided they had to finish before it was too late.

As the end credits rolled, Pamela got up and went into the kitchen. Cecilia smiled knowingly. She knew she was playing the extra on this occasion. But it did not bother her.

Bill was lost for words. He just hoped this was all going to lead to what he had earlier envisaged. The sexy message of the movie was loud and clear. But where did Cecilia fit in?

Pamela swiftly answered that when she returned from the kitchen with a tray of ice cubes and took his hand.

"Let me show you the rest of the apartment..."

Bill just couldn't believe it was finally actually happening. All this expectation and now they were really doing it.

Pamela was firmly in control. Bill knew his place the instant she peeled off her skirt and blouse to reveal a turquoise set of silk lingerie.

As she undid the belt of his trousers, he felt like her pupil once more. It was a nice, secure response. He was unsure. He wanted to be led. She seemed so powerful. So strong. He just did as he was told.

In the first few moments, Bill was embarrassed by his own nudity. But he soon shed his inhibitions as Pamela explored every part of his body in the dimly lit bedroom.

The partly empty ice cube tray was on the bedside table. Bill had smothered the freezing cold pieces all over her body. He was fascinated by the erectness of her nipples when he touched them with the cubes.

He was pushing them gently over every curve, then licking the watery remains with his tongue in a really teasing fashion. It was driving Pamela into spasms of excitement. It was the only time Bill ever got anywhere near being in complete control.

He stopped to put the ice cubes back in the tray, desperate to actually make love. He understood the importance of foreplay but he really wanted the real thing. Each time he tried to stop though, she would insist he carry on with the ice cubes. She wanted him to put them in her mouth and drip tiny droplets onto her body – just like in the movie.

It was time for Cecilia to go. She could well imagine what was going on in the bedroom next door. She had to pass the bedroom door to get out of the apartment, so she braced herself. It wasn't that she was shocked by Pamela's seduction technique. More jealous really.

For Cecilia had been equally turned on by the movie, but she had no-one to turn to. As she crept past the door, that was ever so slightly ajar, she could clearly see the two naked bodies entwined and heaving on the double bed. It was an image she would never forget.

At last Bill was discovering the real thing. They were making love on the bed wildly and rampantly, totally consumed by each other's bodies.

It was a brilliant experience. Sex with an older, more experienced woman!

Pamela's appetite for lust knew few boundaries. She was training her "love slave" to do anything she demanded.

In the background, Van Halen's *Hot For Teacher* was blaring out of the stereo system. Reminding Pam of her conquest. How could she ever forget?

Now she wanted sex on the floor. He had to obey as she pulled him on top of her, guiding him into her because he was still clumsy and inexperienced.

As their bodies moved in rhythm on the shag pile carpet, she fantasised about Mickey Rourke. She knew she would reach a climax, just so long as Bill was half as good as Mickey was.

Bill was feeling guilt-ridden. It was a classic schoolboy guilt. He wasn't sure if he could face Pam again after their night of passion. Now he had actually experienced sex, he was not quite sure how to handle it. Should he ignore Pam and hope her husband does not find out? Or would it be better to take the affair a stage further and become her regular lover?

He could not believe that a woman would give herself to him in the way Pam had, without feeling very emotionally involved. He had read about prostitutes and sex on demand. But Pam was not like that. There was only one conclusion to draw: something special must exist between them.

As he stood in his regular place in the corner of the school playground on the morning after he lost his virginity, he felt a strange combination of elation and depression. The joy of that sexual experience was being mellowed by the ongoing feeling of guilt.

But then he snapped out of it when he sensed Pam's eyes upon him from the other side of playground. This time she was coming towards him, rather than holding back by the double doors like before. As she approached, the other two Musketeers moved away, instinctively aware of the relationship between their best friend and his teacher. Pam had been rehearsing this moment all morning. Now the time had come.

Bill did not know where to look at first. Pamela had obviously been crying. The mascara around her eyes had smudged and she looked a different person from the passionate vamp of just a few hours earlier.

They talked in low, almost whispered tones, to avoid the prying ears of the other children standing nearby.

"I want you so badly Billy," uttered Pamela.

Bill did not know what to say. She was proclaiming

her love for him.

"I've got to have you the whole time. I don't want anyone else. I want you."

Pamela was weeping slightly throughout, but she still had that air of authority about her. The teacher in charge. There was no way he could refuse her anything. If she wanted just him and no-one else than that was fine by him.

There was something wrong though. She seemed to be building up to it. As if she had some other motive for her tears... but he couldn't be sure of it. It did not take long for him to find out.

"We've got to get rid of Greg. It's the only way."

Bill reeled back with shock. Maybe he wasn't hearing her correctly? But Pamela was being deadly serious. She wanted Greg out of the way and she ordered Bill to do it.

The car was parked in a narrow lane off the main highway. It was eight o'clock in the evening. The windows were heavily steamed up and the car was gently rocking – only slightly – from side to side. It was just enough so you would notice if you were standing right by it.

Inside, Pamela and Bill were making love. It wasn't as comfortable as the first time. But it was just as passionate.

"Bill. If you really loved me..."

Pamela wanted her young lover to prove his commitment to her. Bill was in a daze. He had just turned 16 years of age, and now his married girlfriend was briefing him on how to kill her husband. In between gasps she said:

"Make it look like a burglary. Steal a few thing from the bedroom... There's some jewellery in there... The cops will think Greg walked in on the burglars... It's going to be so simple... I don't want you to do a messy job. It's got to be clean and quick... Use a

78

gun then you won't mess up the carpet."

She was ordering the assasination of her husband but her chief concern was her new lounge carpet.

"And don't do it in front of the dog. I don't want him scared."

Pam always said she preferred animals to humans – now she was proving that point beyond any doubt.

Despite reservations Bill was getting what he always wanted – real sex from a woman who really knew how to perform. If he had to carry out certain, well, unsavoury tasks than so be it.

He wanted his lessons to last forever.

Vance Lattime was tip-toeing silently down the stairs of his home, desperate not to wake the rest of the family. As he made his way across the lobby to his father's study, he wondered if what he was about to do was really going to be worth it.

Only a few hours earlier, his best friend and fellow Musketeer Bill Flynn had persuaded him and Patrick Randall to carry out the cold blooded murder of Pamela's husband Greg.

She had been with all three of them when the plan had been discussed. She made them believe it would all be so simple. Vance was not so sure. But Bill and Pam were most persuasive. They knew that Vance's father had a vast collection of firearms at his home.

As the teenager gently opened the glass case and eased the .22 pistol out, he hesitated for a moment. For the price on Greg Smart's head was a mere £2,400 each. That was the amount Pamela had promised Bill that he and his friends would receive from Greg's life insurance. The only condition was that they made sure he was dead.

As he stood inspecting the daunting array of weaponary on display, Vance knew he had made The Musketeers' pledge of honour – and that meant he

79

was committed.

Bill, Vance, Patrick and their driver Ray Fowler were motoring up the freeway towards Derry. They were visibly nervous. They were having to face the reality of the situation – and it was terrifying them. As Ray drove, Bill briefed the other three on the roles they had to play.

No-one was listening properly. Their powers of concentration were all but gone. These were not cold, professional killers. These were four schoolkids who had come under the spell of one determined seductress.

"Shit. Let's turn around," Bill was back in control. Thinking clearly for a moment, he realised the enormity of their task. He could see the ludicrous side of the situation and it was time to take stock of it all. Time to reassess his true feelings for Pamela. Perhaps she was using him to kill her husband? Maybe she would just drop him like a stone the moment the murder was committed?

For the first time, Bill had his doubts about the relationship which had picked him up and swept him off his feet.

"I'm sorry. We just got kinda lost. I couldn't remember which street you lived in."

It was a feeble excuse from Bill and he knew it. But it was all he could do in the circumstances. Vance and Patrick were cowering with him outside the front door to Pam's apartment. They were almost more scared of her reaction than the prospect of murdering someone.

Pamela was indeed furious.

"You don't love me. You got lost on purpose," she was screaming at Bill, totally ignoring the presence of the other two boys.

He was frightened she was going to ditch him. That would mean the end of all that passion. But at least it might leave him with a clear conscience.

Above: Christine English who mowed down and killed her lover Barry Kitson outside the *Live And Let Live* pub in Colchester. *(Left)*

Innocent: Tracey Ann Waugh

Guilty: Kim Jervis

Guilty: Lisa Ptaschinski

Guilty: Tracey Wigginton

Above: The four accused women in the lesbian vampire trial.

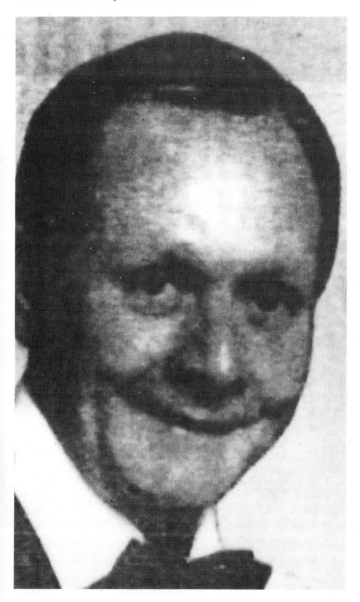

Below: Lesbian vampire victim Edward Baldock

Above: Teacher Pamela Smart used 16-year-old pupil William Flynn *(Right)* to coldly kill her husband Gregory Smart

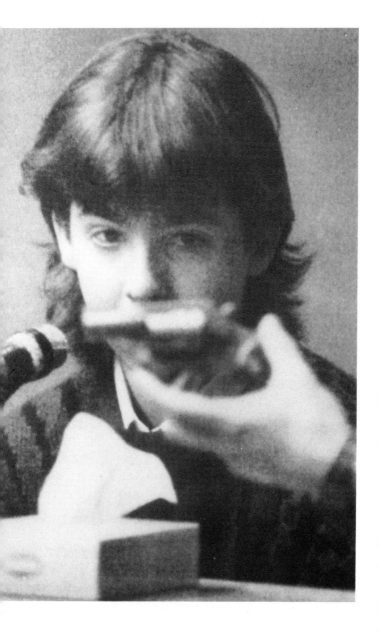

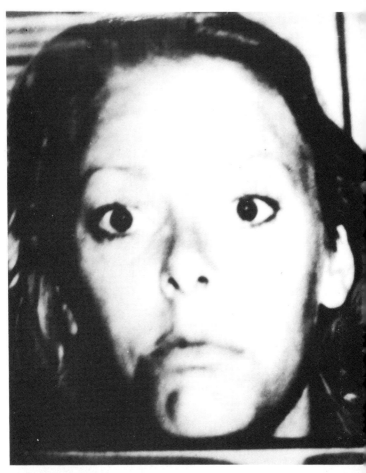

Above: Florida serial killer Aileen Wuornos and *(Left)* two police photo-fit pictures of her before her dramatic capture.
Right: Some of Wuornos' alleged victims.

Charles Carskaddon

Douglas Giddens

Troy Buress

Gino Antonio

Peter Siems

Charles Humphreys

David Spears

Richard Mallory

Above: Poison Pie Killer Susan Barber

Bill was half hoping that perhaps this *would* be the end. He was worried about a lot of things to do with this illicit relationship. It all seemed so dangerous. So risky. But the over-riding guilt always dispersed the moment he set eyes on Pam. Remembering the love making they had enjoyed seemed to lull him into a false sense of security. It was all so easy.

She started to stroke Bill's neck. She was going to get her way. No matter what it took. The two other boys looked on embarrassingly as their media studies teacher kissed and caressed her pupil in front of their very eyes. Pam was well aware of the presence of those other two. She led Bill into the kitchen and told them to let themselves out...

Soon they were making love all over the house. On the sitting room floor. On the staircase. And finally in the bedroom.

Pamela's initial anger at Bill had now transformed into lust. Her fury about the failed attempt on her husband's life was making her more frantic.

Bill could barely handle it. She was oozing with sex. She did not remove her clothes for the first bout of love making – not even her black patent leather stilettos.

She was tearing at him wildly. Wanting more. And more. And more.

By the time they had both climaxed, Pam was like a different person. All the anger had subsided. She had let it all flow out of her system during the love making. She felt immensely satisfied.. for the time being.

Gently, she stroked his chest and looked at him lovingly, as they relaxed together in her double bed. But that nagging feeling she wanted something was coming back to Bill. It was the same feeling that he had when they lay on the back seat of the car a few days earlier.

He knew exactly what was on her mind.

"You've got to try again. This time make it work. If you don't, we shall have to stop seeing each other."

The chilling reminder made Bill's stomach turn. He wanted her so badly. Before, he had hoped the whole crazy scheme would just go away.

He should have known better.

In their Derry apartment, Greg Smart was tidying up before Pamela's return from a late evening school meeting.

He wanted so desperately to make up for the confession which had so upset Pam. He knew it was wrong to have slept with someone else. It was just one of those things. He still loved Pam and he wanted to show her how much. Now, he was looking forward to a great celebration that would wipe those bitter memories out forever.

Greg was so engrossed in his thoughts he did not even notice the smash of a rear window at first.

As the three hooded figures crept through the bedroom towards the lounge, Greg was just thinking who to call next on his round up of friends for the party.

When The Three Musketeers burst in they took Greg completely by surprise.

"Take anything you want." He wasn't going to argue with three men and a pistol.

Bill was feeling elated. The gun. The power. The power to order someone about. Just like Pam did with him. He felt in control of his own destiny for the first time in his entire life. He knew he could get Greg to do anything he wanted. Well, almost anything.

"Give us that ring scumbag."

He wanted that ring more than anything else. He wanted it to be his forever some day.

For a few seconds, the whole scenario was reduced to a farce by Greg's response.

"If I gave it to you, my wife would kill me." One of the other boys sniggered.

Bill and his fellow Musketers were flabbergasted. His wife wanted him dead – and he really did not have a clue.

"Just give us it."

Bill tried to sound menacing. But to no avail. Greg was adamant.

He had just signed his own death warrant.

Bill cocked the hammer on the gun.

"Get down on your knees. Now!" yelled Bill Flynn to his lover's terrified husband.

He pointed the gun at the back of Greg's head and uttered three simple words:

"God forgive me."

Greg Smart fell to the floor silently.

Bill and his two fellow Musketeers beat a hasty retreat...

She looked stunning dressed all in black. The seamed stockings added just that hint of sexuality, at a sombre occasion. She was even wearing the same black patent stiletto's that she had kept on during her last bout of passion with Bill.

This was the funeral of Greg Smart, and his grieving widow was putting on an Oscar winning performance. Head down, she looked heartbroken as the wooden coffin was mechanically lowered into its final resting place in the ground. The so-called Maiden of Metal was melting the hearts of her family and friends, gathered around the graveside.

As they heard the priest refer to Greg's tragic death at the hands of unknown assailants, she shed a tear and dropped a bouquet of red roses onto the casket before it was covered up with earth.

"God rest his soul..."

Back in the playground, the Three Musketeers were in a daze. They still couldn't quite believe what they had actually done.

The newspaper headlines had come and gone. Pamela Smart was still grieving at home – crying those crocodile tears. The whole operation seemed to have gone like clockwork. Now the teenagers wanted to collect their money. It seemed like a job well done.

But they were all starting to drop their guards.

The bragging at school began. Word started to get out that maybe Greg Smart wasn't killed by burglars after all.

"He was worth more dead than alive," boasted Patrick Randall to one classmate.

It was the talk of the playground. The place where, all those months ago, the whole train of events had been set in motion.

It was now only a matter of time.

Vance Lattime was feeling really distraught. He had just woken up after having an horrific nightmare, in which he kept seeing the face of Greg Smart over and over again. It was a vivid image. Lifelike to the extreme, and it really scared the teenager.

He, more than the other two Musketeers, was constantly filled with a sense of guilt that wouldn't let go. While the other boys waited for Pamela to get in contact and hand over their "fees", he was starting to question the whole horrific episode.

At home, his parents thought it was adolescent girl trouble that was causing Vance's depression. The problem was certainly with the opposite sex. But this was no girl. She was a murderous, manipulative woman.

His parents tried in vain to help him over his anxiety. But no amount of appeals would work.

He couldn't keep this evil secret locked up inside his mind for much longer. He knew that other kids were talking about it at school. He was sure the police would come knocking some day.

Then, one breakfast time, he snapped. Breaking down in floods of tears he poured out the entire incident to his stunned parents.

Vance's father went straight to the police.

Pamela took the news of the arrest of The Three

Musketeers and their driver very calmly. She certainly was not going to be panicked into a confession.

As she sat in the once happy matrimonial home in Derry, with her best friend Cecilia, she seemed in a remarkably cool state of mind.

"Who are they going to believe? A 16-year-old, or me with my professional reputation," she said confidently. "I'll get off, don't worry. I'm never going to admit to the affair."

Unluckily for Pamela, she did not notice the electronic tape recorder that was strapped to Cecilia's back...

On March 22, 1991, at a court in Exeter, New Hampshire, Pamela Smart was found guilty of masterminding her husband's murder. She was sentenced to life imprisonment.

Bill Flynn, Patrick Randall and Vance Lattime all admitted killing Greg Smart. Their life sentences were reduced to 28 years in exchange for their co-operation in helping the prosecution of Pamela Smart.

4

PMT

Christine English hated the mornings.

There was always so much to do. Get the kids ready for school. Make sure they ate some breakfast. Do the beds. Tidy the house. A never-ending stream of chores.

And then there was Barry.

Once both her sons had departed for school, she had to nursemaid him through the morning. In some ways, he was more like another child than her lover.

They had been together for four years. But sometimes it felt like four hundred. Their love for each other veered from hatred to total infatuation – and there was no knowing which way it would end.

All her friends kept telling her she was mad to set up home with a man six years her junior, but Barry kept Christine feeling young. When he wanted to be, he could be the most loving, caring person in the world.

She didn't want to listen to what everyone was saying. So long as the good times were more frequent than the bad, she was happy.

Lately, however, she had begun to wonder whether it really was all worth it. Barry had turned to drink in a big way. It started with beers every night in the pub but, in the past year or so, he had found a taste for vodka.

Nearly every night he would end up drunk or close to it. Sometimes he was amusing company when he was tipsy, other times he turned into an out-of-control monster who would strike real fear into Christine.

Barry's problems lay with his work. Like so many self-employed people he was under enormous financial strain. He owned a franchise to a bakery. Although the business was doing OK, it wasn't bringing in the return Barry had once hoped for.

Life had turned into a constant battle for him. His

only way out was the bottle. When he was drinking none of the stresses and strains, however large, would enter his mind.

In the pub of an evening, he would sit at the bar, talking to his drinking partners about everything except his business. It was a great way to avoid the tensions. Drink was the great escape.

When Barry got home to Christine each night, he would start to sober up and realise that what he was doing was merely a smokescreen for his problems. Underneath it all, he was well aware that he couldn't just carry on pickling his brain in alcohol.

He had to do something to sort himself out. But how? Christine knew the answer, but she didn't know how she was going to convince Barry. Many years before, after the birth of her two sons, she had noticed her moods swinging enormously in the space of just a few hours. At first she just dismissed it as temporary post-natal depression. The man she was married to then had not helped. He wasn't interested in her "women's problems".

"What are you on about woman," he'd grumble, an uncomprehending scowl on his face. Their marriage was already crumbling, so compassion did not come high on his list of emotional priorities.

Christine was desperate to break out of the constant moods that were starting to make her life miserable. Sometimes she would get so het up she would start smashing up cutlery. Throwing it around the kitchen in an inexplicable frenzy.

Afterwards, she would try to explain to her husband why it had happened. But he didn't want to know.

"He just did not care. A woman's place was clearly defined in his little world and the sort of problems I had were the sort he did not want to talk about," explained Christine later.

Things got worse and worse at home for Christine. The moods became more frequent and less controllable. It was as if there was a different person inside her, trying desperately to get out and cause havoc.

After one particularly nasty fight with her husband, she threw a plate at him. He struck her. That was it. She had to do something before it was too late.

So Christine turned to Transcendental Meditation. It was the mid-seventies. Hippies had come and almost gone – yesterday's beatniks were today's married couples with 2.2 kids – but TM was a relic that had survived the fickle swings of fashion.

It was also the life saver Christine had been looking for. At first, she attended group meetings where everyone would sit and meditate. Learn to relax in a way the modern world rarely allows you to.

Christine was given her own mantra. It was a call-sign awarded to her by her teacher. A name that no-one else in the entire world should ever know – or be called. Her teacher warned her of the dire consequences if she ever revealed her mantra to anyone else.

Within weeks, she began to feel better. Just meditating for fifteen minutes every morning before breakfast and just before bed seemed to calm her so much. She was starting to look inside herself more. To understand the powers that were making her so tense. Appreciating the evil influences that were contributing to her unhappiness. Christine was starting to find an answer.

It had given her hope for the future and made her far more tolerant and understanding towards Barry's drink problems than she ever would have been with her husband.

When Barry's boozing became excessive she knew she would have to use her TM experiences to help him escape from his problems – just as she herself had done all those years before.

"In any case, Barry wanted it. He was desperate to sort himself out," explained Christine.

One night he wept in her arms, after a particularly outrageous drinking bout, and begged her to help him find the same sort of contentment as her.

He refused to attend a TM session. He wanted

Christine to teach him. No-one else was trustworthy enough. He was like a child in that way, feeling he could not do it in front of strangers. Immature reservations aside, he was desperate to rid himself of his problems before they cost him his life.

Naturally, Christine was troubled by all this. She felt that he should attend proper classes but she knew something had to be done quickly, otherwise it might be too late. What she feared most of all was that superstition about the mantra. He wanted her mantra. Nobody else's. In fact he insisted that Christine shared that name with him as a pre-condition to learning TM.

Barry needed to be helped so badly. He wanted to sort himself out and Christine loved him.

Reluctantly, she agreed to tell him. It was something that would haunt her forever.

Only the night before, they had had such a great evening together. It had been like old times really. Lots of cuddles. Lots of love. Lots of security.

Christine had felt, for the first time in many months, that maybe they could survive together. Barry was meditating regularly with her now. It actually seemed to be working.

Maybe all that superstition about the mantra was nonsense. Perhaps he really would start to live a decent life again. Barry had started to take the TM as seriously as Christine. Every morning they would meditate together. It was having a calming influence. She hoped it would start to divert him away from the drink.

She had gone to sleep that night feeling really optimistic. It certainly made a change.

But the next morning, Christine felt she was back at square one. All that happiness and contentment had disappeared to be replaced with a searing feeling of tension coming from deep inside herself.

However, Barry was not the instigator this time.

The cause of her depression was far more simple,

although just as tragic. Christine was about to start her menstrual cycle – and she felt awful.

Over the years, Christine had got used to suffering really badly. The TM had helped enormously but PMT was still something she dreaded. While many women manage to carry on their lives virtually unaffected, Christine really couldn't cope.

That pre-menstrual stage would build up until she felt like snapping with the tension. In the week or so before her period she would suffer from splitting headaches, swelling parts of the body, pimples on her skin and incredibly tender breasts.

Headaches are often referred to as the body's all-purpose distress signal. They alert you to the fact that something is wrong. In Christine's case, they were throbbing and excrutiatingly painful. Like a hot knife going right through the temple.

Swollen breasts are often a woman's only symptom of Pre Menstrual Tension. But, in Christine's case, they were just part of the agonising scenario. Any hug or pressure was painful. It made her sound irritated, even when she was not. And it didn't help in any relationship with an ignorant man.

Then there was the weight gain and bloating that often accompanied the PMT. Sometimes she would put on as much as seven pounds – all as a result of her body's retention of water.

Her skin also became pink and blotchy. Boils and cold sores were frequent occurrences for Christine. These would affect her confidence and, in turn, could make her even snappier.

Worst of all, though, was the clumsiness. Things were always falling out of Christine's hands. She was forever walking into furniture and knocking things over. Most of the time she would blame herself for her awkwardness. That would put her under even more pressure. Her previous husband and now Barry never truly understood why.

There lay Christine's biggest problem.

The men in her life just never seemed to appreciate the pain and anguish she went through. They just dismissed her behaviour as "bloody irritating". Never bothering to really try to think about what was happening inside her body.

She suffered constant anxiety or panic attacks. She felt unloved, irritable, always on the defensive. She would lash out at people for no reason and find herself bursting into tears at the slightest provocation. Even when Barry bought her a present, she would scream at him for no apparent reason.

Then there was the depression. Moodiness, no interest in people or important events, lack of energy, lack of concentration, forgetfulness, insomnia. It all seemed to gang up on Christine and no amount of TM could completely cure her of it. But at least it relaxed her enough to make her believe she could cope.

When she meditated, her body seemed to float away from all the tensions surrounding her. For a precious quarter-hour, she could lose herself in a sea of mysticism. It was the ultimate escape. Sometimes, she wished she could do it permanently.

But the moment she woke up on December 16, 1980, she knew it was going to be a very difficult day – thanks to PMT.

That tense feeling was in her head as she grappled for the alarm clock. It could only get worse.

At least she would have Barry for support. Surely he would be understanding about her problem this time? He had witnessed her foul tempers enough in the past. When she tried to explain to him what was going on, he started to appreciate the anguish she went through every month. But it was clear that he did not really understand.

On this particular morning, Barry wasn't in such a good mood himself. Although he had happily soothed Christine the whole of the night before, resulting in a pleasant evening together, he had something he wanted to tell her. And he didn't think she'd like it. She'd only been up a few minutes and she was already very stressed out.

As she meditated in the corner of the bedroom that morning, the TM helped ease the anxiety, but she still had the whole day ahead to cope with.

They meditated together, hoping a 15 minute trance at the end of the bed might be the answer to both their problems. But Barry had not been concentrating properly. Christine noticed he had other things on his mind.

The anticipation of the argument he was bound to provoke was already making Barry short-tempered – and he hadn't even told her yet.

He'd let her get the kids off to school before he broke it to her. Otherwise, she would really go to pieces – and that would not be fair on the children.

Barry had a sense of right and wrong. Maybe that was why he was so worried about telling Christine his little secret. In the time they had been together, she had proved to be remarkably possessive. She didn't like any other female even so much as looking at Barry.

He was her's – and no-one else's. That was her attitude and she was sticking to it.

Even when he began drinking more and more and staying at the pub until almost midnight, Christine still regarded him as her property. She was always wary of the predators circling around him. She knew she had to keep a pretty close eye on him.

But Barry was not so keen. He liked the idea of being attractive to other women. It was good for his ego. Besides, it didn't have to mean he slept with them. Being admired is a far cry from infidelity.

He didn't like her possessiveness. It intruded on his freedom. Stopped him being a lad about town.

"I'm going to meet another woman tonight."

Barry spluttered out the words as hurredly as possible. It was as if he knew he had to tell her but was hoping she wouldn't hear him.

Christine heard him all right. She looked up from the breakfast table at her handsome lover. She was momentarily stunned. What the hell was he saying?

They had just enjoyed one of their best evenings together in months and he was now telling her he was going out with another woman.

She was numbed. He wouldn't do that. He couldn't! Why did he want to hurt her? What right had he to treat her like this?

The tension increased by the second as his words began to sink in. Christine could feel the tightness in her stomach as the adrenaline pumped around her veins, making even her finger tips stiffen with anger.

She began to shout at Barry. How could he do such a thing? Didn't he love her? Bastard. Bastard. Bastard.

She would not let him. It was as simple as that. She would not allow him to see the other woman. He would have to make his choice. If he chose this woman then he may as well not bother coming back that night, or any other for that matter.

But Barry was adamant. He wanted his freedom. She could not stand in his way.

He stormed out of the house.

"I am going to run him over. I am going to run him over."

Christine English kept repeating it to herself over and over again. The elderly woman at the other end of the line was understandably perturbed – she was Barry Kitson's mother.

"I am going to kill him. I am going to run him over and kill him."

Christine was adamant. The strain that had been building up inside her all day was fast reaching breaking point.

She had eaten nothing but half a sandwich at lunch-time. For a woman who suffered from severe PMT this was madness. All medical researches on PMT have long agreed on one thing – skipping meals can often worsen the symptoms. The irony is that cutting back on food is a classic response to tension and unhappiness. But the lack of food, when nourishment is sorely needed, can be particularly hazardous.

It was mid-afternoon and Christine was already at the end of her tether. She had to tell someone what she felt – so why not his mother?

Mrs Kitson knew that things between them were not good and that her son was partly to blame, but she listened in horror to Christine's threats.

Christine couldn't concentrate on anything. Her mind kept going back to Barry. She wasn't going to let him betray her with that woman. Not tonight. Not any night.

At home that afternoon she was close to tears as she prepared tea for her two sons on their return from school.

How could he just announce his decision like that? How could he be so uncaring? After all she'd done for him.

Christine sat with her head in her hands wondering what she should do about it. In the back of her mind she kept recalling the words she shrieked hysterically at his mother: "I am going to run him over. I am going to run him over."

Maybe that was the answer.

By the time Barry got home in the evening, Christine felt her life had been systematically broken into little pieces. Everything she relied on to help her through times of crisis had vanished without explanation. The foundations had been dismantled from beneath her feet.

When he walked in, she tried to stay calm but it was no good. She could not bottle up the anger and bitterness she felt toward him. And to make matters worse, he was still determined to go ahead with his date with another woman. They were heading for an inevitable collision.

"How can you do it? How can you?" She broke the silence within minutes of him settling down in an arm chair in the living room.

"I've had enough of this. I'm off."

Barry made for the door. Desperate to find an escape

route away from the constant pressure being applied by Christine. He took the only course of action he knew – and went straight to the pub.

The *Live And Let Live* was the perfect retreat for Barry Kitson, and it had a particularly pertinent name for him that night. It was the sort of place where he could lose himself in a sea of alcohol. Somewhere to forget his troubles. A pub where he could be himself.

With it's beige, nicotine-stained walls and swirling red carpet, the Trueman's Ales pub was typical of the sort of bar found in a provincial English town. A dart board offered the only exercise of the day to any regulars.

Barry took up his stool against the tatty pine clad bar – it gave a clear view through the window to the car park outside.

When Christine turned up that evening, she didn't even have to go into the pub for Barry to know she had arrived.

She walked in and tried to nag at him in front of his drinking mates. He was embarrassed and intensely irritated.

"Leave me alone woman."

He did not want to know. In any case, he still had that date with the other woman to go to. Christine knew that only too well, but she was determined to try to do something to stop it. But the more he drank, the more obsessed Barry became with his inflated idea of freedom. Really, he wanted to see lots of other women the whole time. This was just an excuse to start playing around. Deep down, they both knew that.

Christine really did care about his welfare. She wanted him to come home and sleep off the drink. She hoped he'd forget about the other woman and they could start afresh in the morning.

"Well. If you won't come home, I'll drive you there," Christine finally offered.

It was a bizarre way to respond, but she was convinced that so long as she was near him there was a chance he might give up his plans for the night.

The journey was strained. After all, Christine was driving her lover to meet another woman on a date. Her motivation was bewildering. Most wives or lovers would have kicked their partner out long ago. But Christine lived in hope that they would enjoy a normal, peaceful life together.

The anxiety was building up inside all the time. She was shaking with tension. She was making herself suffer.

When they arrived, Barry got out of the car without uttering a word and walked towards the pub where his secret lover was supposed to be waiting.

As Christine sat in the car outside the pub, it really began to dawn on her what a fool she was being.

Why had she allowed herself to drive him to meet another woman? How could he humiliate her so much?

She sat in the car outside the pub with her eyes closed. Trying to clear her mind. Trying to get a hold of herself. See sense. This was all so ridiculous.

She loved him so much, but what on earth was she doing waiting for him? He was probably inside there holding the bitch's hand while she sat in that car just a few yards away.

People kept walking past her car, wondering what she was doing. She ignored their stares, determined to wait for him however long it took.

After nearly thirty minutes Barry emerged. He was alone. She felt a surge of relief go through her body. He had been stood up for his date. Christine was ecstatic. Barry was furious.

She saw it as a victory. He looked enraged. It was a humiliating climb-down. He was the one who looked a fool now. He had been let down by one woman. Now he had to face the full wrath of another.

Even the drink was beginning to wear off. Even the headaches had been transferred to him.

In the car there was a tense silence. Christine was still outraged by his insulting behaviour. But at least she had her man back. Barry was sulking. It was inevitable they would end up rowing. He called her a bitch. He reckoned she was sneering because she was so satisfied at his failure to pull.

In truth, Christine was far from satisfied. She was angered by his remarks. He was trying to turn the tables on her. Make her feel guilty about the fact that he had a secret rendezvous with another woman.

Her head was throbbing with pain again. It felt as though a tight band of steel was squeezing her skull. Bright light slammed into her eyes, loud noises hammered at her ear-drums, the lightest of touches felt they would bruise. To top it all, she felt nauseously dizzy.

It was Barry, however, who cracked first. He grabbed her hair, slapping her viciously across the face. She pulled the car up and started to fight back. Desperate to hurt him. To make him pay for all the awful things he had done to her.

She blasted the horn.

"Get out... get out..."

Barry carried on hitting her. But then he noticed they had just pulled up near another of his favourite pubs. He got out of the car. Slammed the door and marched off towards the entrance.

He warned her not to follow him. He said he just wanted to be left alone or "I'll call the cops."

Barry must have sensed the devil lurking inside Christine's mind as he walked away.

Christine was shaking with fear at her own rage. She felt incensed by his behaviour. Hurt. Fury. Hate. She had all those feelings going through her head. She had to stop him treating her like this. It could not go on. She kept remembering the warnings of her friends and family. "He's a bad type. What are you doing with him?" they used to say.

She felt an urge to drive after him. To punish him for all those hurtful things he had done. Flatten him into a bloody pulp forever.

She started up the car and drove after him. She wanted to damage him.

As the car approached him, he turned and faced

her. Defiant. Full of bravado.

She looked into his eyes and realised she could not harm the man she loved, so she pulled away and just drove around and around Colchester instead. She needed time to think. She had to get a grip on herself. But the heartbreak of the situation just would not release it's grip on her. One moment she felt compassion and love for him, the next she would feel a burning desire to make him suffer, just as he had made her suffer.

Christine thought that, by driving around, she might be able to work off the aggression. She had been so close to killing him. She had to get that feeling out of her system.

But Colchester has only a small core. Soon, she found herself driving past pub after pub that she knew Barry would go to.

It was inevitable that she would come across him wandering drunkenly out of one. She drove through the town's one-way system. Then she signalled right, back onto the dual carriage way that skirts the edge of the town centre.

It was a repetitious journey. The constant driving was soon interupted when she spotted Barry.

Christine immediately felt that uncontrollable surge of tension returning, when she laid eyes on him.

She stopped the car by him and they began arguing. This time, it was a ferocious row with no limit to the insults they were hurling at each other. All the time, Christine could feel the knots in her stomach tightening.

The enormous stress was exacerbating the symptoms of PMT. She desperately needed to find a way to ease her pain. All that meditation had helped. But, as she sat there, she realised it had not really gone to the root of her problems. The break-down of every meaningful relationship she'd ever had.

Why did she feel so bad? Why did all this have to happen now, just at the most crucial time? Why couldn't she just close her eyes and wake up somewhere pleasant instead of sitting in that car fighting?

"Just go away!" Barry was yelling at the top of his voice now.

Christine felt a strange compulsion to chase after him. She wanted to wind the argument up even more. She wanted it to reach a crescendo from which there could be no return.

Barry was already at breaking point. He seemed about to explode as he sat in the car next to her.

Without any warning he hit her on the head with his hand. It was a short, sharp movement. He did it again. This time smashing down on her arm instead.

She tried desperately to fight back, but he was far too strong for her. They were virtually wrestling inside the car now.

Then Barry drew out his ultimate weapon. Something that would hurt her more than any punch. The threat to end all threats. Something he knew she dreaded.

"I never want to see you again."

He slammed the car door shut and walked off.

She watched him for a moment. In her terrible state, everything seemed distorted with the streetlights and shadows and colours from the buildings and roads all converging on her, rushing towards her as though they would smack the windscreen.

Then she realised the car was moving. She felt herself press down on the accelerator.

I am going to run him over... I am going to run him over. Then a little voice inside her head said. I'm hungry! But it was too late for that now. The only thing she could feed on was revenge.

It was meant to be. Never tell anyone the name of your mantra. It will only bring misery to your life.

He knew her inner-most secrets. Now fate would take a hand and punish him for that knowledge.

Run him down! Run him down! Flatten the bastard!

The evil little voice had to have it's say.

Christine watched Barry as he half walked, half stumbled along the street.

Do it. Go on. He deserves it!

Barry was about to cross the entrance to Sainsbury's. He never got there.

She felt the urge to press harder on the accelerator pedal. She tried to pull her foot up, but the twitching became even worse. She wanted to slam her foot hard down.

It's so easy. Bye bye unhappiness – just one small step...

Barry helped make up her mind. He turned and, looking straight at her, thrust two fingers into the air. Fuck you, they said, you wouldn't dare.

Christine took a deep breath and pressed her foot down as hard as possible on the accelerator. Just a little bump to show him. That'll shut him up.

Barry didn't believe she would actually do it. She didn't have it in her.

As he stumbled across the poorly lit entrance to Sainsbury's, he turned and saw her face. She certainly looked determined. But she wouldn't actually kill him. He'd test her bottle. And laugh at her when she slammed on the brakes.

The front of the car hit Barry with a huge thud. Then he was swept on to the bonnet.

The bulk of his body lolled against the windscreen.

She felt no emotion. Just a determination to finish off the job properly. She could have stopped there and then. He was already badly injured. Instead, she kept her foot full down on the accelerator and mounted the pavement before smashing head-on into a telegraph pole.

The impact of the car jolted Christine out of her intense trance. She heard her lover groaning. The man she had slept with just ten hours earlier. The man she had just tried to kill.

He was pinned between the lamp-post and the car bonnet, his right leg was almost severed.

"Get it off me. Get it off me." His voice was slight and agonising.

"Get it off me. Get..."

He was fading by the second.

Christine English sat for a moment behind the wheel of the car, unable, for a second, to absorb the enormity of what she had just done. Then hysteria took over. It was all so unreal.

"Please, please tell me it's not true. Please God, it hasn't happened."

Christine stood by the side of the car now. She kept telling herself she only meant to frighten him. She did not want to do this.

Two weeks later Barry Kitson died in hospital.

Christine English was given a conditional discharge for twelve months after pleading guilty to manslaughter with diminished responsibility when she appeared before Norwich Crown Court.

Before deciding to free her, Judge Justice Perchas said, "There is no course of treatment which can be prescribed for you. But now you are aware that a dramatically minor affair like eating properly is of the utmost importance."

5

Poison Pie

She wrapped him in her arms, burying his face in her dark, curly hair. For a moment they rocked back and forth, looking intently into each other's eyes. Then she trailed her tongue from his earlobe to the nape of his neck, stopping every few seconds to kiss and suck his young skin. She licked an imaginary line up a few inches before coming to rest at his ear. There, her tongue probed deeper and deeper. It felt as though she was touching his ear drum, exploring every centimetre before sucking the air from it gently and sensuously.

She was in control. She, the mother of three young children, could do anything she wanted with him. He was six years younger – a virgin until he met her.

Next, she nibbled his earlobe. Five, maybe six, times. He was far too excited to be able to count. They were both standing by the end of the bed, waiting for the right moment to fall backwards onto the soft mattress.

She kissed his chest, circling each nipple with her tongue before biting the end. He winced. The pain was sharp, but pleasant. She looked up at his face to see his reaction. His eyes looked glazed and distant. Her silky lips teased each breast, before sucking in hard.

Domination. That's how she liked it. It gave her more pleasure than anything else.

Her lips started moving further down now, exploring every contour of muscle beneath skin. She ran the tip of her tongue from side to side just above his penis. The lovely, beautiful power of the tease. So near and yet so far.

Finally, after what seemed like years, she went lower. Sucking. Biting. Sucking.

Susan Barber was in ecstacy. She was satisfying her young lover in a way that he could not resist. She could do anything she wanted to him and he would just whimper for more. He was so inexperienced – anxious to learn and receive.

They both fell on to the bed. She paused for a moment, making him lie on his back because she wanted to decide when it was time. Until then, she would tease and caress him to within a flick of a finger before orgasm. Each time his breathing reached fever pitch, she would pull away momentarily, just to make sure he did not come.

Soon she would let Richard get what he so badly wanted. But, until that moment she would continue pushing him to the limit. Watching him squirm with a delight tainted by exasperation.

The unmistakable sound of the front door slamming came from downstairs. Susan stopped dead. It was followed by a crash of cutlery in the kitchen.

"Shit! He's come back early."

Susan jumped up and grabbed her nylon housecoat from the end of the bed. She could hear her husband coming up the stairs. He had heard something. He was going to find them.

Richard was panic stricken. He was not as fast off the mark as Susan. Also, he had peeled his clothes off in her front room when they had first started kissing.

"*Shit*!! He's seen the clothes on the floor."

The bedroom door burst open. Michael Barber was steaming with rage. He had come home early from a fishing trip because of bad weather. It was nothing compared with the storm of fury about to erupt in his house.

There was no point in either of them denying it.

Richard was standing completely naked by the wardrobe, desperately trying to find something to put on. But then he could hardly take out a pair of Michael's trousers!

Susan's nipples pressed hard against the nylon of her housecoat. It was obvious she had nothing else on underneath.

"You whore."

Michael Barber grabbed at her coat. He wanted to rip it off her, humiliate her. She evaded his grasp and made a dash for the door.

But Michael was not going to let matters rest there.

"Come here you slut. Come here!"

He yelled abuse at Susan, then he turned his attentions to Richard. Only two days before, the two men had played on the same side in an Essex inter-league darts match at *The Plough*. Now, that same "friend" stood before him stark naked after just having made love to his wife in his bed. This was the same man he had bought a pint of bitter for so often. The same man he had congratulated on getting a bullseye. The same man he had encouraged to be patient with the darts team scorer.

"She's not too good at adding up mate. But her heart's in the right place."

"She" just happened to be Susan.

"You fucking bastard."

Michael stood there and looked at Richard's pale and plucked body.

"Pathetic. Fucking pathetic."

Richard stayed silent – afraid to inflame the situation. Not really knowing what to say.

"Now get the fuck out of my house. Bastard."

Michael tensed his fists in anger. This was an insult to his manhood. His pride. His reputation. He had to do something about it.

"I'm going to kill you."

He lurched towards Richard, just missing him with his right fist. Still completely naked, the slightly built lover made a move for the door. He was vulnerable and highly embarrassed, but he had to get out of that house if he valued his own life.

"Come here you fucking cunt!"

The two men came thumping down the stairs.

Richard slipped, rather than ran, down the stairway. Losing his balance every two or three steps in a desperate bid to escape Michael's clutches. In the hallway, he stopped for a moment, but it was a ridiculous idea. There was no way he was going to pick up his clothes from the front room *and* escape without a beating. They still lay scattered across the carpet where – less than an hour earlier – Susan had so amorously removed them. Richard lunged for the front door.

Michael was gaining on the younger, lighter man. Richard struggled with the front door lock. It was one of those yale-type double locks. Almost as difficult to open as to close.

Susan pushed him out of the way and opened the lock for him in one quick motion. She blocked the way while Richard made a run for it. Michael barged his wife out of his path, sending her flying to the floor.

As he reached the front door step, he saw Richard's naked form desperately fiddling with the garden gate. He gave up and hurtled over it in one precarious leap.

Michael knew he would get away. He stopped chasing and watched as the nude figure ran four houses up Osbourne Road, then went up the pathway to the neighbouring house.

Michael looked at his wife.

"Now it's your turn bitch..."

He shut the front door and hit his wife across the face.

Michael and Susan were barely on speaking terms the next morning. By the time he left the house to go to work at the nearby Rothman's factory, the atmosphere had got so tense that she had genuinely feared for her life.

The previous night he had beaten her black and blue. She couldn't face another thrashing. Rather than inflame the situation any further, she kept quiet. Praying he wouldn't pick a rematch with her.

Within minutes of watching her husband leave their modest three-bedroomed semi, she found herself thinking about Richard. He kept her going. She wanted to be with him the whole time.

There was not a lot of other happiness in her life at that time. Richard satisfied her craving for physical love. Sex was something that had been missing from her marriage for at least five years. Now she had got her sense of adventure back. She loved to feel that she was doing something exciting. Daring. Naughty.

She always felt so good when she was with him. He made her feel ten years younger than her twenty-nine years – and that was the best part of all. She could relive her lost youth by behaving as irresponsibly as she wanted.

Now, her husband had gone off to work and she wanted her lover once more. She stood by the telephone in the hallway, wondering if she should call him. Would he even want to see her again after what happened yesterday? Perhaps he'd want to finish their affair? After all, he must have been pretty scared. But then again he had left his clothes. That gave her an excuse to call.

She picked up the phone.

Susan and Richard lay next to each other in bed. Both were entirely satisfied. Content for the first time in days. Physically drained from an hour of energy-sapping love making.

"He's mad you know. One day he'll kill you," said Richard.

Susan knew her lover was right. She had long harboured an intense hatred for her husband. The beatings. The verbal abuse. The lack of affection. The list of reasons why their marriage was in shreds was endless.

She had promised herself she'd leave him. But she'd never plucked up the courage to actually do it. Now, however, it was different. Her infidelities were out in the open and he would become even more violent towards her. He wouldn't be able to understand her need for sex. He'd given it up so why should she have it? That was just the way he saw life. Revolving around him.

Now his pride had taken a battering. The whole street probably knew what had happened that night. A naked man runs out of their house with the husband in hot pursuit. And he just happens to be the boy who lives with his parents a few doors up the road. The evidence was there for everyone to see.

It would be the talk of the neighbourhood, if not the whole of Westcliff-on-Sea, by now. Susan didn't care. Her need to be loved far outweighed her reputation amongst a load of petty, nosey neighbours. But he would.

As she lay there next to Richard, she began to realise that maybe there was only one solution to the problem. "Kill him before he kills me."

She got out of the bed and put on her clothes. Richard looked disappointedly at her. She beckoned him to come with her. They had some very important business to attend to.

The Barber back garden was not exactly an impressive example of superb horticultural skills. A few flower beds dotted about the place. A scrap of grass in the middle, badly worn by the antics of three young children. A few toys scattered haphazardly beside a climbing frame in the corner.

It was a garden all the same. And nearly all the gardens in Osbourne Road had one thing in common – a shed. They were a vital part of keeping up with the Joneses. The sort of shed you had was a definite reflection of your wealth. Neighbours would frequently glance along the rows of gardens, comparing their own outhouse with those in every garden for at least 100 yards in each direction.

Michael Barber's shed wasn't perfect. But it certainly

had a lot of character to it. He had built it with his own fair hands out of slates of wood he got when he worked for a firm of landscape gardeners. About eight feet square, it had another very important role to play besides being the place where he kept all the tools and utensils. It was his very own very private retreat. A place where he could get away from everything. Where neither the children nor the wife could bother him.

He would often spend hours fiddling with bits of car engines in the shed, happy in the knowledge that no-one would disturb him. It was the perfect place to escape if you happened to live in a town like Westcliff-on-Sea.

Now, Susan Barber was trying to find out if that shed held the ultimate escape route for her.

With Richard by her side, she was trying to find the Paraquat poison she knew her husband had left in the shed a few years back.

She remembered the day he got it, back in the seventies, because he brought it home from work and used to go on and on about making sure the kids got nowhere near it. They were younger then.

"It's a killer, this stuff. Just remember that."

Susan had never forgotten her husband's warning.

She took great care as she heaped tablespoonfulls of the powder into a small pill bottle.

Richard smiled as he watched her.

Susan had taken full heed of her husband's warning by using a bottle with a child-proof cap. You didn't want it getting into the wrong hands, after all.

Susan made an effort for Michael when he came home from work that evening. She wanted to make amends. Start all over. Try and make the next few weeks as bearable as possible. They might be his last.

She made his favourite dish for tea – steak pie. If there was one thing that just about brought a smile to his face, she thought, it was steak pie.

It needed to be cooked for hours beforehand, to make the meat as lean as possible. Michael would never allow her enough money to buy the good meat. She had to make do with that tough stuff that the butchers virtually gave away. But, after simmering for a long time, no-one could really tell the difference. At least that's what Michael always said.

Earlier that afternoon, Richard gave her a warm embrace as they stood by the cooker. Together, they were hatching a plan that could give her the perfect way out of an awful marriage.

She picked up the plastic pill container, untwisted the lid and sprinkled the powder into the gravy she was mixing on the stove.

"How much do you think? Is that enough?"

"No. Put some more in. He won't be able to tell the difference."

Richard hugged his lover, giving her an extra tight squeeze as she dropped most of the contents into the gravy.

He won't humiliate me ever again, she thought.

Michael was not particularly impressed with his favourite dish when he eventually got home from work. He was still seething with anger about the events of the day before. Furious and unforgiving. How could she expect him to just forget the fact that, only twenty-four hours earlier, he had come home and found her in bed with one of the neighbours? What difference could a bloody pie make?

Mind you, he was starving hungry – and that steak pie did smell delicious. Susan always cooked great pies.

It must have covered three quarters of the white plate. The yellowing, crusty pastry contrasting with the dark brown, almost black, colour of the beef. The peas and boiled potatoes were like an afterthought really. Barely making an impression, compared with the vast quantity of pie.

Susan watched him pouring the gravy over the food.

She found she just could not keep her eyes off it. For a moment, Michael looked up at her quizzically.

"What you looking at woman?"

Susan smiled and got back to her own dish of food. She never did like gravy anyway. She always made it especially for her husband.

Michael was a messy eater. He tended to hold his knife and fork like two drum sticks and shovel the food into his mouth. Usually, Susan would grimace with disgust while watching him stuff his face. But this time she actually found herself enjoying the sight of him eating. Munching, and then noisily swallowing, each gigantic mouthful. It was a lovely sight.

She tried to keep her head down in silence. That was the way it was normally at meal times. Every so often, though, she allowed her eyes to travel discreetly towards his plate of food, where he was feasting on that very special pie.

It didn't take a lot to get Susan excited when she was in a room with an attractive man. Her husband had long since stopped having that effect on her. However, as she sat at the kitchen table, watching Michael devouring his food, she felt a strange tingling sensation rushing through her body. She kept fidgeting in her chair in the hope it would divert his attention from her obviously excited state.

Crossing her legs one moment. Uncrossing them the next. She had to clench her teeth to stop herself from giggling. She could not believe he was actually eating it without a word of complaint.

Richard had said he wouldn't taste a thing. She hadn't believed it. She thought it would surely have had some sort of aftertaste.

But her grotesque lump of a husband was loving each and every mouthful.

"Got any more of this stuff on the go?"

That was the nearest he had come to a compliment
rs. She took his plate and piled on yet more
sparse sprinkling of vegetables and sloshed the

whole lot with gallons of gluey gravy.

Her breathing had quickened. Would he notice?

No. He was too busy filling his fat stomach

"What's for sweet then?"

Susan snapped out of her trance. It was probably just as well.

She served up his pudding, happy in the knowledge she had just sentenced her husband to a slow and agonising death.

Susan was irritated.

It had been three days now and there had been no sign of it taking effect. She lay in bed next to her husband wondering if she would have to give him even more Paraquat. Richard had warned it would take a few days.

She could not stand the waiting. Not knowing if his cast-iron stomach had already managed to flush every trace of poison out.

How much longer would it take? She had given him a massive dose. Surely he would start to suffer soon?

Maybe they should have cut his brake pipes instead. That would have been much faster and simpler. None of this cooking and waiting around.

As she lay there, she became aware that her husband was stirring. She kept her eyes tightly shut in case he realised she was awake.

It was the middle of the night. He could hardly breath. His throat felt as if it had a layer of carpet clogging it up. His chest was pulsating with pain. What he did not realise was that his lungs had been rapidly turning hard and leathery – making it more and more difficult for any air to get through. Then he started to get awful stabbing pains in his kidneys.

He got up to get a glass of water. But the liquid just made the stinging sensation even more unbearable. He felt as if hundreds of tiny daggers were travelling through his body, stabbing his insides at every opportunity.

Every few moments, his body would twitch with discomfort as the stabs became more and more frequent.

"Susan. Wake up. I'm in fucking agony. Call the doctor."

Susan Barber thought she was dreaming at first. But no. Her husband's anguished face looked very real.

"At first, we thought it was pneumonia Mrs Barber."

The doctor was full of sympathy for Susan as they stood by the hospital bedside. She had called the ambulance when Michael collapsed on the bathroom floor.

Slowly. Ever so slowly. She dialled the emergency services. She didn't want to hurry in case the end was near.

Wouldn't it be great if he died here and now, she thought for a moment. But he was still struggling for life when the ambulance men eventually turned up. Maybe it would be even easier if he died in hospital. Less mess. Less questions. Less suspicion.

In any case, nearby Southend had a perfectly pleasant hospital. Good clean wards and caring nurses. What more could he ask for? But then Michael Barber was hardly in a fit state to appreciate the nurses!

The poison was now definitely beginning to kill Michael Barber. To him, it must have felt as though a psycopath had been let loose inside his body. Travelling to every corner of his system, ruthlessly mutilating every living organ for no apparent reason.

Now, the doctor in the hospital sounded hesitant about the illness. Perhaps he suspected it was poison? Maybe they were trying to put her to the test? Watching her reaction for any signs of fake concern. Had they found traces of poison in his blood stream already?

For just a brief moment, Susan was worried. But then she thought, where are the police if they suspect? She glanced around her. No-one was approaching with handcuffs. No-one was even looking in her direction. She knew she was still in the clear.

112

The facade of concern for her husband's well-being should not slip for one moment. She had to keep up the pretence. She must not give them any clues.

The doctor at Southend Hospital looked most concerned. Susan wondered what he was about to say.

"We think it may be a condition called Goodpasture's Syndrome. It's a rare nervous disorder that breaks down the body's internal mechanism."

Susan was confused. Luckily her confusion helped make her look even more like a heartbroken wife, whose husband was on his death bed.

It was 1981. The AIDS epidemic had not really begun to take its devasting toll on the western world, otherwise the doctors probably would have suspected he was an HIV victim.

Susan was touched by the doctor's concern. It was so nice of him to be so caring. If only he knew she really did not give a jot.

Susan just hoped and prayed he wasn't such a good doctor that he might find out her husband had been poisoned. Worse still, he might even save Michael's life. That really would not do.

"We recommend he is transferred to a special hospital where they can keep an even closer eye on him."

She did not care where it was, so long as he hurried up and died.

At the beginning of June, Michael Barber was transferred to the Hammersmith Hospital in West London. It had been less than one month since Susan had laced his gravy with Paraquat poison.

On June 27th, he died a dreadful, painful death. The cause was given as pneumonia and kidney failure.

It was only a small service. Susan, the kids and a handful of friends and relatives.

He would have wanted it that way.

Whether he would have welcomed his wife's lover, Richard, with such open arms was perhaps not so certain.

113

However, Susan needed him there. He was her support – even though they could not stand too close together in case other people noticed.

Instead, they looked at each other longingly as the coffin trundled slowly into the crematorium oven. The organ music played a timeless hymn in the background and the oak casket slid through the curtain. The final memory of her husband. Burning in a box of wood.

She had insisted on the crematorium. It meant there would be no body to re-examine. No doubting doctor could exhume his corpse and find fresh clues. He was gone forever. No-one would find out.

Now she and Richard could go and get drunk and celebrate. The £16,000 pension and the £900 a year allowance for the kids should take care of them for a while. It had all been so easy.

At Hammersmith Hospital, Professor David Evans had a nagging suspicion about the death of Michael Barber. He had carried out a detailed post mortem the day after his death. He even took test samples from the body. Blood, urine, everything he could think of, just in case there were signs of Paraquat. He removed vital organs and ordered them to be preserved in jars and kept in storage.

All the signs were there. It had to be. Why else would a perfectly healthy 35-year-old man collapse and die.

Professor Evans reckoned the tests were a mere formality. Once the results arrived back, he would contact the police and tell them to arrest the wife immediately.

He was stunned when they did come back from the National Poisons Unit. There were definitely no signs of Paraquat poisoning. The Professor could not believe it. But he had to take the word of analysts. Even so, he still felt a nagging doubt.

Something about the case did not add up.

114

There was nothing he could do about it now. Death was through natural causes – the death certificate said so. He would have to drop the case.

"Aren't you bothered what the neighbours think?"
There were times when Richard was shocked by Susan. She just didn't seem to care. She had no pride. He may have been younger than her, but she was the one with the irresponsible streak. The one who was wild and untamed.

It was the day after her husband's funeral, but she couldn't wait a moment longer to have him to herself. She insisted he bring his belongings around and move into the house. He had no choice.

Susan had got away with murder. Now she could enjoy her life for the first time in years. She didn't give a damn what people thought. No-one suspected her. It was the perfect crime. Now she wanted her reward – and it came in the shape of Richard. He was the young lover she did all this for. He was the man she wanted in her bed.

Richard, however, was not so keen. It had all started as a casual affair. He'd been swept up by the whole thing.

When they first met at *The Plough*, he didn't even realise what was on her mind. After all, he was a kid still living at home. She was a happily married mother of three children.

Richard had always lived with his parents. Sheltered from the outside world, he had never even slept with a girl. When his mates in *The Plough* told him that she had a definite soft spot for him, he thought they were kidding.

When she asked him round one afternoon while Michael was out working a day shift at the nearby Rothmans factory, he went in all innocence – convinced that any fantasies he had about her would not actually come true. She wanted him to fix the fridge. He was more than happy to oblige.

The boys at the pub had already told her he was

still a virgin. The idea of seducing an innocent really appealed to her. Richard was even more willing to oblige when she offered to take him to bed.

Six months later, however, he was starting to grow tired of her. She had taught him so much about sex. But now he wanted to try it out with someone new. He didn't want the full time commitment of a live-in relationship – especially with a woman who had just murdered her husband. But Richard was weak and impressionable. That was why she had got him in the first place. He didn't have the courage to tell her what he thought. He just accepted the situation and moved into her house.

It was obvious it would never last.

Professor David Evans was growing more and more fascinated by the Michael Barber case. He kept going back to his findings and re-examining the facts. Just in case he had made a mistake. He was looking for something more that would tell him for certain his suspicions were unfounded. He just would not accept the situation. It kept niggling at him. He knew he had to drop the case from his full-time agenda but that did not mean he had to forget it altogether. However hard he tried, he couldn't come up with an explanation of why Barber actually died.

The inquest might have concluded it was natural causes but Professor Evans knew otherwise. Even if it wasn't poison, it was certainly a fascinating case and he thought it would be intriguing for some of his colleagues to study it.

With the furthering of medical science in mind, he decided to call a conference, the following January, of all the doctors involved in the case – more than six months after the death of Michael Barber.

At least they could swap notes and compare findings. Something that might help save lives in the future.

Susan Barber was bored. She was fed up with being

the dominating one in her relationship with Richard. Why couldn't he make a few decisions for a change? Surely he could start acting like a real man rather than a wimp? Maybe it was time to swap him for a more mature model? At least Michael had had a bit of character. Shame, in a way, that he was no longer around.

She laughed at her own ludicrous notions. Michael was the last person she wanted back on this earth.

They were drifting apart. More and more, she was thinking about other attractive men. It was how she felt when she was married to Michael.

It was time to end it – and get out there and start enjoying life once more. Wasn't that exactly what she told herself when Michael was still alive?

Richard was only too happy to go. Back to his parents, four doors away. They might as well have been a world apart.

Susan needed a new man if she was going to satisfy her never ending lust for life. Meeting them was not easy in Westcliff-on-Sea. A small, rather drab Victorian seaside resort, it was filled with pensioners living out their last few years. Hardly the sort of place for a merry widow to find an energetic young lover.

Susan was going crazy with frustration. She needed the comfort and support of a man. But, most of all, she needed the physical pleasures. That was what kept her sane. She thought of sex frequently. She needed to satisfy that demand. But how could she do that in a place like Westcliff?

Strangely enough, she eventually found the answer in citizen band radio. Susan had hardly touched the CB set since Michael's death. Now she had an urge to switch it on. She would find herself a man. First, she had to think up a call sign.

"Nympho" seemed appropriate.

Steel erector Martin Harvey always considered himself fit and healthy, but even he was having trouble keeping up with Susan Barber. They had met in the pub only a few hours earlier but it was clear from the start what Susan was after. Everyone knew what Susan liked to do with men.

"She'll eat you for breakfast mate," said one helpful soul.

In the pub, she cuddled up to twenty-year-old Martin and told him exactly what she wanted. Richard had gone. She wanted him to share her bed with her, give him her own unique taste in pleasure.

Within seconds of arriving at the house, she had ripped his clothes off and got down to business in front of the electric fire. The first time was pretty traditional but, three hours later, she still had not stopped.

The bathroom. The kitchen. The toilet. The spare bedroom. There was no room left in the house where they had not done it.

Then Susan decided she wanted to try something new.

Leaving Martin lying naked on the bed, she walked over to the corner of the room and switched on the CB transmitter.

"Nympho here..."

She soon found a willing partner. She told him to turn up the volume and listen. She put the microphone on the table by the bed and got back on top of Martin and started to make love to him.

She whispered in his ear not to make a sound. She wanted her CB pal to think she was having sex with him on the airwaves.

She moaned and sighed. Then she turned her head towards the mike and said: "Can you hear me... I'm coming... harder... harder... I want you to come too."

A few days later she was back on the CB again.

"Hello. This is Nympho calling Magic Man. Do you read me... over?"

Her provocative name would attract the right sort of man.

"Magic Man" turned out to be Rick Search. He had

built up quite a rapport with "Nympho" – now he wanted to meet her in the flesh.

The garage mechanic liked the sound of "Nympho". He had that feeling she would live up to her name. He had been surprised, but hardly complained, when she suggested a date. He agreed without hesitation.

Most of the lonely women who broadcast on the CB airwaves tended to be grandmotherly figures just looking for someone to talk to. But "Nympho" wasn't after a friendly chat. She positively oozed sex down the microphone.

She had decided it was a great way to meet new lovers.

Rick had no doubts what to expect when he called round at her house in Osbourne Road.

He was not disappointed. The magic was definitely there.

Susan was really enjoying the freedom her CB romances allowed her. Most of the men were just interested in one thing – and that suited her. She loved the excitement of meeting men on blind dates. She would wait at the window to her house and watch them arrive. If they were not her type then she would simply pretend to be out.

They'd soon go away. Convinced that "Nympho" must have been a crackpot who never meant a word of all the sexual innuendo she had spoken over the airwaves.

The merry widow was having the time of her life.

It was now January, 1982.

At Hammersmith Hospital, Professor David Evans had assembled the team of doctors who worked on the strange case of Michael Barber. Before them lay a bizarre collection of the dead man's organs and bodily fluids, which had been pickled and stored away.

The doctors began a minute, piece by piece examination of every bit of evidence. They looked at slides that showed Barber's body. They studied the photos

119

of his organs. Then they disected the actual remains. It was a macabre gathering. But Professor Evans believed it had to be done.

The doctors concluded there were still many unanswered aspects to the case – but there was not enough evidence to re-open it. What baffled them was how Barber could have consumed the Paraquat in the first place. Since 1975, it had been deliberately manufactured with a pungent smell. No-one could have taken it without almost immediately vomitting from the awful aroma.

But, as a final jesture, they all agreed that leftover blood and urine samples should be sent to Paraquat manufacturers ICI and the National Poisons Unit.

Some of the medics argued that tests had always proved negative. But Professor Evans just wanted to make doubly sure...

Two months later, the results came back.

This time they were affirmative. Michael Barber had been poisoned. The original tests had never taken place. All those months earlier, a laboratory technician had wrongly informed Hammersmith Hospital the tests were negative.

In April, 1982, Susan Barber and Richard Collins were arrested in Osbourne Road. On November 8, 1982, at Chelmsford Crown Court, Susan Barber was sent to jail for life after being found guilty of murdering her husband.

Former lover Richard Collins was sentenced to two years for conspiring with Susan Barber to kill her husband.

6

Killing Daddy

Wet Willie's was the kind of bar you never went into alone.

The shoebox-sized saloon was filled with denim-clad drifters and hard nosed bikers with no place to go.

"They were the type of people who would bust your head open for a buck," according to regular Dick Mills.

Night after night the same crowd of no-hopers would fill the cramped bar playing pool, drinking beer and raising hell. It was the sort of place you read about, but tried to avoid. A room full of renegades existing on incredibly short fuses.

It was situated slap bang in the centre of Daytona's most notorious red light district. The Florida city made famous by the one of the world's most dangerous motor cycle circuits, was a haven for bikers of every race, creed and religion. But, unlike the immensely wealthy speed heroes of the track, most of these enthusiasts had little more to offer life other than a passion for their machines.

The Daytona race was held just once a year – but these people lived their entire existence in the beach-side city.

Many of them scraped a living out of manual labour. Others just gave up hope and survived by sleeping rough and stealing a meal every now and again.

Dick Mills was a stocky sort of guy with lots of tatoos up each arm. He was different to most of the crowd. He had tried desperately to get out of the vicious circle of violence and excessive boozing by marrying Connie – a local girl with a good background.

Dick had been through a hell of lot in his life.

A Vietnam Vet, he witnessed the horrors of war first hand. It was a time that haunted him still, made worse by the realization that the awful carnage he'd seen in South-East Asia was also happening much closer to home. Murders. Rapes. Muggings. They were all everyday occurances in Daytona.

Dick's first marriage had failed miserably, because he had got caught inside that short-sighted bikers' world. Now he was trying to make amends and start again with a new wife and, he had hoped, a new life.

Connie seemed the perfect kind of girl for Dick. He was gone 40 now and knew he wouldn't have many more opportunities to find happiness. When they married in the summer of 1990, it really had seemed the perfect match. But, just four months later, Dick was wondering what had gone wrong. He had dropped his biker image. She wanted them to settle down. Be responsible. Lead a careful life.

It didn't last. There were too many temptations around for Dick to handle.

Connie had kicked him out because the arguments seemed never ending. They rowed about the dishes, the TV, the money. You name it, they battled over it. It all proved too much for either of them to stand.

Now his life was back where it had started. No future. No job. No money.

He slouched into *Wet Willie's* to drown his sorrows.

It was Christmas, 1990. For Dick, that was simply an excuse to get drunk.

Country music blared out from the bar's jukebox in the corner. Two bikers dressed in oil stained denims played a round of pool at a furious rate – spurred on by alcohol and a need to act macho. Three Hell's Angels talked about engine bearings and the inner workings of their Harley Davidsons. Every now and again, prostitutes with hard, gaudy faces walked into the bar, cast a glance at any lonely looking men and then "home in" to do business. For these girls, it was a damn sight more pleasant inside *Wet Willie's* than cruising the sidewalks of nearby North Ridgewood Avenue. There, the girls were often raped or attacked after plying for trade with a motorist – who just happened to want to make a woman suffer. They all dressed in either skin tight jeans and stilettos or pencil-thin skirts, often made out of slinky leather or rubber. It was a uniform really. They had to attract the eye of every passing male and the glistening shininess of their outfits spelt the message out loud and clear. An advertisement that read: "I am for sale. Why not buy me?" Then, as a curb crawling driver slowed down to inspect the goods, they would make eye contact. Nine times out of ten that would guarantee success.

Dick Mills wasn't interested in paying for sex that night. For one thing he was skint. And, more importantly, his mind was on other things. His disastrous marriage. His failure in life. His failure as a man.

As he supped at a can of ice cold beer, he was only just aware of the music being played. If a woman had come up and sat right next to him at that moment, he probably wouldn't even have looked up.

He eventually awoke from his problems when one of his all time favourite country songs broke through his stupor. Johnny Paycheck's Take This Job And Shove It had a certain aptness to his own current situation. It brought a wry smile to his face.

He swivelled round on his bar stool towards the juke-box. Dick wanted to see if a real soulmate had put the record on. He was starting to feel sociable again.

There, sitting next to the jukebox, was a blonde woman, all alone.

It was the first time Dick had noticed anyone the entire evening. But then he could not help seeing this particular girl.

She was crying and singing to the droning music all at the same time. She looked up and smiled briefly at Dick.

He smiled back – immediately attracted by her face and her grief.

He examined her for a moment. Even amongst the bikers and the prostitutes, her outfit seemed sexually charged. She was wearing a black leather, tight fitting all-in-one motorcycle jumpsuit. It had a red stripe down each side. Showing up the contours of her body as she sat down at a table on her own.

Aileen Wuornos was heartbroken. She had also just split up with a lover. They had enjoyed such passion together. But now all that was gone.

Every time she thought of the outrageous sex, it made her cry because they would never enjoy each other again. They had parted, split up for good. Now, she realised just how much she needed her lover. She'd been the dominating one, but they both got the same pleasure out of their relationship. If only she had appreciated that at the time.

But then love between two women is often more powerful and possessive than any heterosexual affair.

Dick was perturbed. He had come into *Wet Willie's* to forget his troubles, not pick up a woman. But the alcohol had gradually begun to ease the pain and now he felt the sort of urges that had nothing whatsoever to do with a broken heart.

He watched the woman by the jukebox closely.

And she knew he was watching her.

As her tears began to subside, she too started to feel something. It was the need to be loved by someone. Anyone. It didn't really matter who.

However, Dick was a shy sort of bloke underneath and he couldn't conjure up the courage to even ask this girl if she wanted a beer. He kept getting up off his stool and then sitting down again – unsure how to make the initial approach.

She was gyrating her body to the music now. Slightly rocking in her seat. Squeezing those leather clad thighs together. Thinking of Tyria Moore, her beautiful blonde lover. Remembering those glorious, hot days when they would spend 24 hours in bed together exploring each other's bodies.

They tried everything together. It was a never ending world of sexual experimentation. And Tyria never objected. She just wanted to please Aileen all of the time.

Dick couldn't help noticing her gyrations. It was quite exhilarating to watch. This girl had real rhythm. She must be one hell of woman, thought Dick.

At the fifth attempt to move towards her, he actually got up and began the short walk to the table, where she was sitting. He was nervous. He did not like rejection. Even though he was there alone, he found it embarrassing.

Aileen was howling to the music and swigging back bottles of beer at an alarming rate. People in the bar had noticed her all right. But they just looked away, bemused. The sight of a lone woman getting drunk was unusual even in *Wet Willie's*.

All Dick could see in the dimly lit bar was the slinkiness of her leather suit in the lamplight. He was just a few feet from her when he heard the leather stretch and rub against the plastic seat as she moved in the chair. It was an exciting sound. As he approached the table, he still did not think he could bring himself to talk to her.

"You got a car?," Aileen broke the silence between them. It was a relief to Dick. She had made the first move. Now he felt the confidence to press further.

"Yep. Sure do,"

As he stood by the table next to the jukebox, the music was now loud enough to trigger nosebleeds in the car park outside.

Finally, he sat down opposite her. She smiled wearily. But at least she did not tell him to get lost.

"You wanna lift someplace?"

Dick looked at the zip fastener at the front of her leather outfit. It was undone just enough to show a hint of her breasts, which were squeezed tightly against the hide.

"Hi. My name's Lee Green. What's yours,?" said Aileen.

Her real name was just one of many deep and dark secrets she would always keep from Dick.

Within minutes, he had agreed to give her a ride to the Greyhound Bus Station in Daytona. It was the place where Aileen kept her belongings – including a well-used pistol.

As they walked out to the car park, Dick's mind was only on her body, so distinctly outlined by the tight fitting black leather outfit. Even when she abruptly refused his offer to open the car's passenger door for her, he thought nothing of it. She was just some women's libber – not a deadly man hater, he thought.

They drove along North Ridgewood Avenue, past the hookers and the drug dealers on every corner. At one point, while they waited for the lights to change, a tall, black prostitute beckoned to them.

Dick noticed how Aileen stared at the street walker, intensely examining her mini-skirted body. She seemed to know her. But then again maybe not. As they moved off, Aileen turned and watched the girl disappear behind them. Dick didn't think much of it. Just another hooker, he presumed.

Aileen's interest had, of course, been sexual. When she saw that girl's shapely body it had, momentarily, awoken her animal instincts once more. She remembered why she had always preferred women to men. Their bodies were so much more interesting.

Aileen was relieved to get a lift – even from a man. But the fact remained that men had ruined her life a long time before...

It had all begun when she was still in her cradle, 33 years earlier in Rochester, Michigan.

Her mother Diane could not cope with baby Aileen and brother Keith, so she turned them over to her parents for adoption and disappeared. The reason she ran away was simple – her husband had a terrifying temper and used to beat her regularly. Later Leo Pittman's psychopathic tendencies resulted in the sex

126

abuse of one child and the suspected murder of another. Aileen's mother was well rid of that evil man.

The next man to ruin Aileen's life was a brutal teenager, who made her pregnant at just 13. He raped her and then denied being the father. Aileen's grand-parents swept the entire episode under the carpet and packed her off to a home for unwed mothers, where the baby was born and then taken away.

When Aileen ran away at 14, it was no surprise that she ended up supporting herself as a prositute. With no home and no family to turn to, she had been living under the shadow of death since the day she was born.

Men were the root of all evil as far as Aileen Wuornos was concerned.

Now she was accepting a lift from a strange man in the middle of a dangerous town. She would never learn.

"Pull over. Pull over now."

The police car megaphone was loud and clear. The patrol car alongside Dick and Aileen was stopping them for a traffic violation, or so Dick presumed.

Aileen was scared. Her fear of cops had steadily increased during the previous 12 months to the point of paranoia. She had a lot to hide. And she wasn't going to stop running now. She wanted to get away.

She felt the cold steel of the pistol inside her over-night bag. In some ways she hoped she would have to use it. Then the end might come more quickly.

Her breathing was uneven now. Aileen was nervous. She watched as the two officers walked around to Dick.

"Tell them to fuck their asses," she hissed.

Dick thought a more cautious approach might be wiser. He had enough problems at that moment. He didn't want any trouble with the cops.

"Hey. Fuck off cops. Leave us alone."

Aileen couldn't control herself. She had to get the first words in.

She gripped the pistol hard in her hand as she spoke. But it was still hidden from view inside that bag.

Dick was taken aback. What the hell was she playing at. It was as if she wanted to get them arrested. Why was she doing this?

"Shut the fuck up will you?" he retorted.

Dick was adamant. Aileen turned her head away in fury. No man could tell her to shut up. Men were nothing. They were scuzzbags. They used women and then discarded them like old packets of cigarettes.

They had no right.

Dick somehow managed to smooth over the cops but he was stunned by her aggressive nature.

"She went wild at the sight of them. Completely crazy. I just didn't understand it at the time," he said later.

But it was only one of the many warnings signs that were to follow.

"Just drive around for a while."

Aileen recovered her composure. They had only been making a random licence check – nothing more.

Perhaps she wished it had been something more, then she could have fired at them. They would have fired back and, maybe, it would have been the end. Then she could have confessed her sins.

Instead, she had Dick to talk to. He seemed all right, for a man.

They soon discovered their mutual bond – the pain and anguish of broken relationships.

"We're both in the pits of hell. You're blown out over your broken love affair with Ty. I'm blown out over wanting Connie back. We're both manic depressives. Insane in a way," Dick told her.

He was absolutely right of course. But Aileen didn't want to tell him how correct he really was.

Later he recalled, "There are two people I've ever met who have met the devil and shaken his hand. One is me. The other is her."

That night, they drove around Daytona just talking. Talking about the heart-ache and the misery of losing the one you love. They compared notes. For Aileen it was a weird experience. She was pouring out all her problems to a man. Perhaps the end was already in sight.

It was kind of inevitable that Dick and Aileen would end up in a motel room together. After talking themselves dry, it seemed a reasonable enough thing to do. They were both lonely and unattached. Why not?

As Dick unlocked the door to the scruffy, slightly stale smelling room at the Hawaii Motel, on South Ridgewood, he was just glad of the company. The sex – if it happened – would be a bonus.

This was hardly a glamorous, romantic place. Five pounds a bed for a night, but neither of them had anywhere else to stay.

Aileen was surprisingly relaxed. It had been a long time since she had slept with a man. In fact, when she was with Ty, she pledged never to screw one of those bastards again. But that was over now. So why not? Dick didn't seem like the others. He actually listened to what she had to say without treating her like some idiot dyke. It made a refreshing change. Most of the men she had slept with either paid money for the pleasure or raped her without any remorse. Now she was with a man who seemed genuinely interested in her. Why shouldn't she allow him to sleep with her?

She started to remove her clothes by unzipping the front of her leather all-in-one jump suit. She knew the outfit turned Dick on and really enjoyed watching him watching her. She felt she wanted to give him some real pleasure. Just this once.

Dick was nervous. Aileen had admitted being a lesbian yet she was about to have sex with him. Why?

He found her attractive but he could not understand if the feeling was mutual. It was impossible to tell what Aileen was really thinking.

Aileen felt the need. She wanted a man. Usually, a woman was enough. But this time she felt different. She knew that nothing could match the satisfaction a man gave in certain ways.

With Ty it had been good. Incredibly good. They had done everything there was to do. But, just occasionally, she yearned for the full penetration of a man. She still wanted to dominate though. No man would get the better of her and the only way to treat them was to make them do what she wanted.

"Lie down," she ordered Dick.

He did as he was told and then began a sex session that was led by only one person – Aileen.

What she wanted she got. Like an animal on heat. Sometimes her sexual savagery reached frightening levels. She didn't care about her partner. It was pure luck if he climaxed with her.

But she kept going for hours. Making demand after demand. Determined to get her own way.

Underneath it all, Dick was just another man – and they all had to suffer.

Hours later, the two lovers lay in bed together, thinking...

"I loved her so much. I'll never replace her."

Aileen was crying tears of love for Ty on Dick's shoulders.

Dick had never experienced such animal passion before. Yet, Aileen still only had one real obsession – her former lesbian lover.

Dick was the last thing on her mind. He was just an object to be used. Ty was different. She was Aileen's life blood. She inspired her to do things. To commit the ultimate crime.

Aileen did that first killing purely and simply for Ty.

It was just a year earlier on December 1, 1989.

Aileen – as usual out of work and out of pocket – was hitch-hiking in the Tampa Bay area of Florida. The previous day she had left the home she shared with Tyria desperate to earn some money. She felt an obligation to provide for them both.

"I've gotta find some customers. Otherwise we can't pay the bills," she told Ty.

With any luck the right sort of guy would pick her up, give her a lift and pay her cash for some fast, impersonal sex.

Electronics repair man Richard Mallory, from the nearby seaside resort of Clearwater knew he faced a few lonely hours on the main US 1 Interstate highway. He didn't hesitate to stop when he spotted Aileen thumbing a lift by the side of the lane. But Aileen did a double-take once inside the car. For 52-year-old Mallory looked just like her father. He would have been about that age as well.

It instantly put her on her guard. After all, he was the man most responsible for her awful life. He was the man who made her wish she had never been born. He was also the person from whom she had inherited the devil.

"You are evil and you will never stop being evil," her step parents had told her. Now, she knew why.

As Mallory started to make polite conversation, Aileen grimaced with disgust. Maybe this was her father? Perhaps he was still alive after all?

Mallory had no idea what was going through Aileen's mind.

"You want to fuck me?" Aileen put all those thoughts of her father out of her mind for a moment. She had business to attend to.

Mallory hesitated for a moment. Was this why he had picked Aileen up in the first place? But then how was he to know what she about to offer?

"Pull off towards the forest." Aileen did not wait for a reply. She was barking orders now.

Mallory just did as he was told.

He was falling for the bait.

They stopped at a wooded area where Mallory parked his 1977 Cadillac.

131

"Get your clothes off first." Aileen was in control of another man. She loved it.

Then she saw her brutal father once more. She remembered the cruel beatings he inflicted on their mom. She thought about those two poor little girls whose life he ruined.

He was there. In the car next to her.

She felt a fierce compulsion to reach into her bag for that pistol. She had always carried the weapon with her in case of trouble with clients.

But now she wanted to destroy all memories of her father.

Mallory was angry she had not yet removed her clothes. He shouted abuse at her. An unfortunate thing to do. She wouldn't take that from men. Not any more.

He was transforming into her father. Bullying and accusing her. Treating her like dirt. He showed no respect. She was just a whore to be used and abused.

As he bent down to take off his socks, she pulled the .22 pistol out of the bag and fired.

The first bullet ripped into his back instantly. As blood gushed from the wound, Aileen fired again. This time it tore into his shoulder blade. She heard the crack of the bone as the bullet passed through.

But two bullets weren't enough. She pulled the trigger again. And then again. And then again.

Five open holes were gapping through his back.

Now she had got rid of her cruel father for good.

Slumped dead over the steering wheel, just as he should be. An ineffectual lump of meat. She felt no remorse for what she had done. She felt no emotion as she shoved his body under a piece of carpet that lay by the roadside. He was a sick, perverted man. She should know. Getting rid of him was doing the world a favour.

In the trunk she found a suitcase, camera and jewellery. It would be enough for her and Ty to live on for weeks.

Now she had the means to survive.

That evening she used the Cadillac to move Ty and her to a new place to live. Her lover chose not to notice the blood stains on the driver's seat...

Back in the scruffy, seedy Hawaii Motel, Aileen was pouring out her heart to Dick. He was understanding and caring. Only too well aware of the agony caused by a broken love affair.

It was strange really. For underneath it all, Aileen knew that she could not kill again, because she no longer had Ty to look after. It was like a compulsion when they had been together.

She had felt obliged to provide for them both – no matter what. If it meant prostituting herself to make the cash then that was fine. If it meant murdering in cold blood then that was fine. She would have done anything to keep Ty.

Like the previous June when the two lovers yet again ran short of cash. Aileen knew it was time to go out and find a victim.

She again chose her favourite guise as a hitchhiker.

It was so easy to get men if you thumbed a lift. When they gave a ride, they always expected one in return.

This time the venue was the windswept and desolate Interstate 95 and 65-year-old missionary Peter Siems slowed down the moment he saw the leather clad Aileen. His fate was already sealed. The *Christ Is The Answer Crusade* worker was about to meet his maker.

As she got into his Pontiac Sunbird, Aileen became convinced once again that her father was behind the wheel.

The evil man had risen again. She would have to finish the job off once and for all. This time, she would fire seven bullets just to make sure.

Siems, turned his back to her while she undressed. He never saw the hail of bullets that hit his crumpled, elderly body. He was dead by the time the second one tore into his spine.

133

Less than 30 minutes later, she dumped his body in a wooded area near an abandoned country road and made off in the Pontiac.

Aileen was ecstatic. She loved driving the powerful coupe and couldn't wait to get back to Ty.

She really believed the memory of her father had now been wiped out forever.

It gave her great pleasure to make Ty happy. A nice home. An expensive car. They had it all now.

Aileen wanted to take Ty off to places like Disney World. It was a means of escape from their hopeless existence. A story book environment where they could lose themselves in fantasy.

For almost a month they motored round Florida on a wild spending spree. Going every place they knew. Seeing everything. It was a happy time for Aileen and Ty. But all good things have to come to an end sometime.

It happened in Orange Springs – a sleepy, sun-blasted state town where the major social event of the year was a summer fete for the local church.

So when two women crashed through a fence in Orange Springs and ran off from the scene, they naturally created a lot of interest. And very generously broke the tedium of a few people's lives. Several witnesses, including a local fire chief and his deputy who rushed to the scene of the accident, chased after the two women to see if they were all right as they struggled along a nearby road.

Aileen told them to "Get lost".

Police traced the car to missing Siems.

Now, the whole state was hot on the trail of Aileen and Ty.

Dick was growing very fond of Aileen.

To him, she was just a lonely, tragic figure – suffering from the after effects of a broken love affair. He had no idea of her past.

He was so taken with Aileen, he even decided to

134

introduce her to his family at a special get-together.

His two daughters had managed to find true marital happiness and he wanted to share his new friendship with them. They were naturally inquisitive to meet the woman who had so completely bowled over their father.

"You see this scar. I got it during a fight with two dykes inside jail."

Aileen was trying to impress Dick's daughter Reveshia.

Not surprisingly, her story was going down like a lead balloon.

This was the woman her father was so smitten by? Reveshia was horrified. Her sister Tammy was even more stunned when Aileen told her tales of her massive consumption of drugs including LSD, PCP and mushrooms.

The problem was age old: Aileen was becoming more and more drunk. Her defences were down and she was doing the only thing she knew how. She was fighting her way out.

She grew more and more obnoxious as the evening continued.

The more uncomfortable she felt, the more she guzzled down the beers. Dick was forced to go out to the liquor store to get her another crate to sustain her enormous drinking capacity.

It was the last straw for Reveshia.

"Just get her out of my home and don't bring her back."

Dick obeyed. He knew that Aileen had failed the family test and it was nearly time to finish their romance.

Next morning, at the same motel where they had first made love, Dick was about to prove to Aileen why men cannot ever be trusted.

Having made love to her all night, he was now explaining why they had to finish.

135

"Here's £25. I'll drop you off whereever you want to go."

It was Christmas Eve. Aileen had no home, no lover and no-one to turn to.

She had committed the ultimate sin over and over again. Now her punishment was beginning.

Aileen headed for the only familiar place left in Daytona – The *Last Resort* bar. Once a thriving beer-and-wine tavern, it had been redecorated by the hundreds of bikers who swamped there each evening.

Bras and soiled panties hung from the ceiling and in the back yard was the "Japanese Hanging Garden" – consisting of motorbikes dangling from every tree.

It was an even tougher place than *Wet Willie's*. But at least Aileen could drown herself in endless bottles of beer without anyone caring.

"Hey man. She's a flat cracker. I'd keep away from her if I were you."

Two men were leaning at the bar studying Aileen, wondering if there was any point in trying to chat her up.

The six foot tall, leather clad barman, Cannonball, warned the men: "She's a strange one. Be very careful."

If he had realised how accurate those words were, then he might not have allowed her to sleep on the porch outside, every evening, after closing time.

She had nowhere else to go.

Cannonball knew she was trying to get away from something but Aileen wasn't telling. She just bawled her eyes out each evening before falling asleep in the plastic covered car seat in the corner of the creaky wooden porch.

In Pensilvania, Tyria Moore was just relieved to get home to her mom. Aileen had been something terrible. She kept thinking about that time she came home and said chillingly, "I just killed a guy." Tyria kept telling herself that Aileen was lying. But she knew, deep inside, that it had to be true.

136

The nationwide TV programme screened the photo fit pictures of her and Aileen – the net was closing.

She was horrified to discover that her ex-lover was the serial killer being hunted in Florida. But she still didn't know what to do until two police officers came knocking at her mom's front door. Soon she was singing to the police to try to help them catch Aileen before she murdered once more.

Sgt Bruce Munster of the Marion County Sheriff's office may have tracked down Moore. But he still hadn't got anywhere near to finding Wuornos.

She was a killer on the loose – liable to strike again at any time. In any place.

It was time to spread the net and begin random surveillance at the sort of Daytona Bars where she might just hang out. One of those bars was The *Last Resort*.

For more than a week, the two bikers sat and watched Aileen sinking further and further into alcoholic oblivion.

They hoped she might leave the bar and lead them to the bodies of some of those men. But she never did. Too sodden with beer to even think about those victims she picked up and slaughtered out there on the highways of Florida.

Instead, she played her two favourite records "Leather and Lace" and "Digging Up Bones" on the juke box over and over again.

They were like the two theme tunes to her life, soon coming to an end.

On January 9, 1991, Aileen Wuornos was arrested by the two bikers – plain clothes policemen – and charged with first degree murder.

Dick Mills – the man who shared five days of lust with her just a few weeks before – is probably one of the luckiest men alive today...

Aileen Wuornos admitted the murders of Siems and Mallory. She was also accused at the time of publication of the murder of at least five other men and faced the death penalty if found guilty.

7

Sisters of Mercy

The screams were blood curdling. Ear-piercing yells of pain. Long screeches that echoed into the night.

Then silence. A couple of minutes of blissful silence. Then, another scream. This time even more horrendous. Even more high pitched. Even more agonising.

Five-year-old Charlene Maw and her sister Annette, seven, were lying in their tiny beds too terrified to move.

When they heard their mother let out another anguished cry, they trembled with fear. Too scared to say anything in case he picked on them next.

Then, once more, there was an eery silence from the kitchen downstairs.

The two sisters hoped and prayed that the beating had finished. That their bullying father had ended his drunken frenzy. They looked at each other across the room, praying that he had given her some respite from the vicious attack.

Maybe he had beaten her so badly she lay unconscious? Possibly even close to death?

The inner feelings of these two little girls were already damaged beyond repair

On that terrible evening, the quiet that then descended on the ordinary looking semi-detached home in the Yorkshire town of Bradford seemed to indicate the worst was over.

The little girls tried to get back to sleep in preparation for the full day of school that lay just a few hours ahead.

Tears streaked down their cheeks as they listened to the unmistakable sound of footsteps clumping up the stairs.

Their father was stumbling drunkenly to their bedroom one clumsy step at a time. Half way up he tripped and cursed the carpenter who had built the damn thing.

Charlene and Annette were shaking in their beds – terrified that his footsteps would stop outside their room.

The door burst open and fifty-year-old Thomas

Maw appeared – an ominous shadow in the doorway. Just a black shape filling the entire entrance. The stale stench of cider filled the air as he stood swaying from side to side.

The girls pretended to be asleep. Their faces screwed up tightly in case he made eye-contact. They could feel his eyes boring down on them. Examining their faces for any clues to whether they were actually awake.

Even through his drunken stupor, Thomas Maw knew his young daughters were pretending to be asleep. A lip-curling smile crawled up one side of his face. Just a hint of his back teeth caught the light shining from the hallway.

The first to feel the back of his hand was Annette. He slapped her across the face.

"Get up. Get up you little bitch. I want to show you something."

Annette could see the hatred in his bloodshot eyes. It scared her. She was confused. Too upset to fight back. Too scared to say "No". As he grabbed her nighty, she felt like a rag doll in giant hands. She could feel the force of his grip as he made her stand to attention. She trembled with cold and fear.

Next came Charlene. Having seen her father assault her sister, she was so scared that she got out of bed immediately. Desperate to avoid the sort of brutal back handers she had just watched Annette suffer.

Little brother Bryn, aged three, was the only one who had been genuinely asleep. But then he was a boy and boys do not always feel the full wrath of their father's anger.

"Get downstairs. Now!"

Maw was slurring his words, spittle flying from his mouth. He kept snorting through his nose. Lost for breath and wheezing one moment, shouting and cursing the next. But the message was loud and clear.

"Get down there NOW!"

Annette and Charlene were petrified. Perhaps he had killed their mother and wanted to show them the body as a warning to them all to behave?

The two little girls knew one thing though — they had to get down to that kitchen as fast as possible if they were going to save their mother's life. He would give her another beating if they did not obey. He was always blaming her for their behaviour.

All three little children rushed down the stairway, desperate to see if their mother was alright. Inside the tiny kitchen, pots and pans were scattered everywhere amongst fragments of broken plates on the linoleum floor. And there on the floor, amongst the debris, was Beryl Maw. A clump of her hair was hanging from her scalp where he had tried to tear it off. Her face was red down one side. But she was conscious. Desperately trying to compose herself so that the children would not see what an awful beating he had inflicted on her.

She could take the punches and the scratches, but when he tried to rip out her hair by its roots, that really drove home the message that she had married a monster. Yet in his more sober moments, Maw would confess that he was jealous of her curly brown locks. It seemed so bizarre for a husband to be envious of his wife's hair. But he actually used to make her keep it short and dyed black. One day she asked him why.

He just screwed up his eyes in fury and shouted: "It's so bloody curly. I wish I had hair like you." For the first time in more than 20 years of marriage, Beryl had discovered what drove her husband into blazing temper tantrums – her hair. It was as frightening as it was ludicrous.

Back in that wrecked kitchen that evening, Mrs Maw was just thankful to be alive. She had glimpsed the other side and didn't want to go there yet.

Annette and Charlene rushed to her and hugged her protectively. They were relieved to see she was still conscious, despite being black and blue from her husband's attack.

They held her tightly. But it was difficult for her

140

to return their affection. Just to squeeze her arms
around the girls was agony. Everything ached so much.
But it was her head that really hurt. It throbbed from
ear to ear. It was unbearable. The pain seared left to
right, right to left, increasing every time she made any
slight movement. When she rubbed her scalp with her
hand she felt the gapping wounds where he had ripped
whole clumps of hair out by the roots.

Frightened Bryn cowered in the corner of the tiny
kitchen. Bemused. Puzzled. He didn't understand. It
was one in the morning. Why had they been made to
go downstairs in the middle of the night? Were they
going some place? He just wanted to go back to his
teddy bears and bed. He was confused. But even he
could feel the tight atmosphere – it was fused with
hatred.

And Thomas Maw certainly knew what it was all
about. That was why he had forced his young family
to come downstairs. He looked into the eyes of his
two daughters. They looked away the moment they
caught his glance. Scared. Appalled by his behaviour.
Disgusted at what had happened. How could he do
such a thing?

They tried to hug their mother even tighter. But he
saw it as an act of defiance that could not go
unpunished. Their look of contempt for him was enough
to ignite a further onslaught.

The look reminded him of his wife. The woman he
had taken solemn vows with twenty years earlier. The
same woman he had just spent the previous two hours
trying to beat to a pulp.

Without warning, he grabbed Beryl by the hair and
pulled her towards him. The children grimaced with
horror. He was starting up all over again.

They couldn't stand to look. But they felt that if
they turned away he would beat her even more
viciously. He wanted them to watch. If they did not,
he might finish her off forever.

Charlene couldn't take much more. She could not

bear the expression on her mother's face. Alternating from a grimace of excruciating agony to a dull, blank, far-away stare.

She tried to push him away from her mother. He simply swiped her to the floor and warned the other two: "You're next if you're not careful."

Then, as if he were a teacher demonstrating to a classroom of pupils, he said: "This is what I do when your mother disobeys me and this is what I'll do to you."

The children winced as yet more handfuls of hair were torn from their mother's scalp. He was pulling with such ferocity that her head was being jerked from side to side. As the hair ripped out there was an awful noise, like splitting cardboard.

"Stop Dad. Stop. Please stop" the girls begged their father. But he was not interested in their pleas. He wanted to make them suffer. Teach them all a lesson – a lesson in obedience.

Then he held his wife's hair with one hand while he smashed her face on the edge of the kitchen sink with the other. Her teeth crunched as they connected with the metal.

The children were screaming now, but he ignored them. Determined to wreak an awful revenge upon the woman he was supposed to adore and cherish.

By the time her head crashed on the sink for the fourth time, Beryl Maw was on the verge of a blackout. She could just make out her three children, standing transfixed by this awful picture of domestic horror.

The pain of watching their faces as he continued unabated, was almost as bad as the physical agony she was enduring. Just to see them being forced to witness this attack was punishment in itself.

She strained to keep her eyes open. Afraid of what he might do to them once she was gone.

Then she lost consciousness.

Thomas Maw had beaten his wife senseless. The provocation? Smiling at him in an off guard moment a few hours earlier.

It was the first time Charlene and her sister Annette had seen their father's brutality – but it was an image that would keep coming back to them over and over again as the years went by.

For once in his life, Thomas Maw was behaving like the true gentleman his wife Beryl had fallen in love with and married nearly twenty years earlier.

They had been out for a meal in an expensive restaurant and she actually felt that perhaps there was some future for them together.

Mrs Maw had endured years of beatings from her husband but somehow never felt the courage to get up and leave it all behind.

There were always so many other considerations. The children. The house. All the things that keep families together through thick and thin.

Now she felt that perhaps it had all been worthwhile. He was making such an effort tonight. He seemed to want to make amends. To win back her love after years of torment. To show that he really cared. But Mrs Maw still had a nagging doubt in the back of her mind.

She had always promised herself she would get up and leave him once the children were old enough to cope. Now, here he was turning on the old charm. The charm that he had used so effectively when they had first met at a dance so long ago. He was a suave airman who had swept her off her 17-year-old feet.

They were married just a few weeks later.

But the Thomas Maw she knew then was unrecognisable now.

Even on their wedding anniversary he had managed to get drunk. But at least he was being nice to her. It made a change.

As they drove home from the restaurant she wondered if he really was going to turn over a new leaf. Perhaps he could change back into the man he had once been.

Beryl felt almost relaxed in his company that evening.

It was the first time in years she had felt that way.

Thomas Maw was feeling happy too. But his mind was on things other than his marriage as he drove along the busy streets in the town's liveliest late night area.

Mrs Maw then noticed the car was slowing down by the kerbside. She was puzzled. What was wrong? Was the car about to breakdown? She looked over at her husband for a reaction. He didn't even acknowledge her.

No. Thomas Maw had spotted two prostitutes cruising along an empty pavement. His wife may have been sitting right next to him, but he wanted those woman. It didn't matter what she thought. She could go to hell if she didn't like it.

He slowed down to proposition them. Beryl Maw could not believe her eyes as her husband rolled down the window and whistled the girls across to him.

"How much?" He asked in a nonchalant manner. The women were almost as surprised as Mrs Maw by his behaviour. After all, how many men stop to pick up a street walker with their wives sitting next to them?

One of them leant over to talk to Maw.

"How dare you." Beryl was indignant with rage. How could he do this after they had enjoyed such a great night together.

The prostitutes took a step back. They sensed an explosion was about to occur. They even had a sympathetic look on their faces. As if to say: "How could this man be such a filthy pig?"

Thomas Maw did not see it that way. Women existed to be used and abused. What right had his own wife to stop him picking up a street walker?

He was infuriated that the two women were now walking away. Enraged that his wife had the nerve to decide whether he should pay two compete strangers for sex.

Maw aimed his fist straight at his wife's face. Her nose exploded in a shower of blood. He followed through with other blows to the body.

144

By the time they arrived home, Beryl Maw had suffered two black eyes, a broken tooth and bruised ribs. Thomas Maw would never change his ways.

"That bloody rabbit has to go." Thomas Maw was drunk yet again. This time he was throwing his verbal abuse in the direction of Charlene and Annette's pet rabbit. He was furious they had built a hutch for the animal without asking his permission first.

The children grabbed the rabbit out of the hutch and ran into the house. But Thomas Maw had decided that it had to die. Grabbing a knife from the kitchen he charged after the terrified little girls. They stumbled as they raced up the stairs to their room. The rabbit jumped out of their hands – straight into the path of Mr Maw.

He grabbed the white, furry creature and gleefully stuck the knife into its belly, twisting the blade menacingly just to make certain. He did it right in front of the little girls, relishing their distress.

The rabbit was dead. But Maw had another grisly surprise up his sleeve. Three hours later the family sat down to a lunch of rabbit stew. He made them eat up every mouthful.

Maw's cruelty towards animals knew no bounds. They couldn't answer back, so that made them even better victims. He would take awful delight in gassing mice and flies in the kitchen oven, watching them through the window as they contorted and twisted.

Worse was to come. They listened to him kicking a puppy to death in his bedroom – all because it had urinated in the hallway. Only a few days earlier it had been given to them as a present.

Many other awful incidents followed but Thomas Maw surpassed even his appalling standards when the children found a frog in the garden. Snatching the creature out of Annette's hands, he took it into the kitchen and beckoned the children to follow him. They were scared. They knew he was about to do something horrible. They also knew they would get an awful beating if they did not do as they were told.

In the kitchen, Maw took out a straw and told the children to watch carefully. They were puzzled. He never bothered to show them interesting tricks normally. In fact, he hardly ever even acknowledged their existance, calling them "stupid bastards" most of the time.

But, looking at his smiley, cheery face, they presumed he was about to act like a real father and play a game with them.

Now he had the children's attention, he placed the straw inside the frog's mouth. Still the youngsters were baffled. They could not work out what he was about to do. He was being so friendly towards the frog all the time, stroking it and loving it. They guessed it was going to be something nice and it made them all feel warm and excited inside.

Maw leant down and put the other end of the straw to his lips. His eyes looked up at the children just to make sure they were watching.

They saw the glint then. The expectant look. But they just thought he wanted to make sure they did not miss the trick.

They watched him take a deep breath inwards. Then he blew with all his might. The tiny frog ballooned up, getting bigger and bigger. It began to look like a toy. Not a real, living creature.

Little Bryn began to laugh. Charlene and Annette did not laugh. They knew by now that what their father was doing was cruel and nasty — the work of a madman.

Suddenly the frog exploded like a balloon that's been fed too much air. Bits of its green scaly body flew across the kitchen, hitting the children with a wet sting. They cried with horror, unable to understand what had driven their father to do such an evil thing.

The girls ran to their room and refused to come down for days. Beryl Maw now knew beyond doubt that she was married to a monster.

On March 27, 1989, Thomas Maw poured himself the first of ten pints of cider he was to consume that evening. Sitting in the front room of his home in Ranelagh Avenue, Bradford, he supped thirstily at the pint glass in his hand. He was feeling tense as usual and desperately wanted to feel the rush of alcohol to his brain.

In a place like Bradford, most men go to the pub for a drink. But Maw's ferocious temper had got him banned from every single one in the area. Those landlords had taken the sort of measures Mrs Maw should have taken years earlier.

The rest of his family were nowhere to be seen. They knew better than to hang about when Maw decided to go on a drinking spree. No-one except his ever loyal wife would even talk to Maw by now. It had just got too much for the rest of the family. Yet somehow, through all the punches and the slaps, Beryl still loved and adored her beast of a husband. She had already endured so much battering that the pain no longer mattered.

"It was fear and helplessness. I had lost sight of who I was," she said later.

Then there were his terror tactics – deliberately intended to warn her who was in control. One night she remembered him saying: "Leave me and one dark night I'll find you and that will be it."

Mrs Maw believed his every word.

But that night, she sat willingly in the living room with her husband as he downed pint after pint. Her daughters kept warning her to keep away from him.

"He's the devil in disguise mum."

Annette was by now an attractive 21-year-old and Charlene fast catching up at 18. They had their own lives to lead. But they always swore they would not leave her to his mercy. That monster would have to leave the house first.

Beryl made polite, nervous small talk with her husband about the weather and the day's news. It was hardly the level of conversation that a married couple should enjoy. More like a meeting between two complete strangers. But she was so anxious to please – even after the awful life she had suffered.

The tense atmosphere took care of that. All the time there was this overwhelming awkwardness. As the minutes passed, she could feel him building up. Getting more and more angry within himself. It was only a matter of time.

But still Mrs Maw sat there, praying and hoping that perhaps they could enjoy a night together. Just the two of them relaxing in the comfort of their own home.

It was something her two daughters would never understand. Why had she let him make her suffer so much? The answer probably lay with them. They were the reason she carried on.

"What do you think of this Margaret Thatcher?" asked Mr Maw. But before his wife had a chance to answer he followed up.

"Bloody *woman* isn't she?"

Maw was spoiling for a fight yet again.

In the kitchen Charlene and Annette could hear the sound of raised voices. They knew it was the first sign of trouble.

Weeks earlier they had promised each other they would not allow his beatings to continue.

"We have got to do something – before it's too late," said Annette at the time.

Now they had to turn those words into action.

"I've had enough. I'm going in there to tell him what I think of him."

Annette had cracked. She could take no more. In recent years, he had started taking it out on her as well as their mother.

She was haunted by all the awful incidents. Like the time she had spent five hours doing a drawing for her 'O' level preparations and he ripped it up into tiny pieces – just because she had smiled at him.

He would beat her regularly calling her "stupid" and "thick".

Now he was about to beat her mother yet again. She could not take it anymore. She had to act – now.

Annette wanted to protect her mother. The only way was to confront the beast.

Ironically, as Annette charged through the corridor towards the front room, she strongly resembled her father. Maybe it was the way she was walking, but she reminded her sister of the way their father looked at his worst.

Charlene had no option but to follow her through the house to the front room. She pleaded with Annette to calm down. She genuinely feared their father could turn so nasty it would prove deadly one day. That day might have come.

The two girls stormed in. The diversion at least gave their mother some respite. An interlude in the cruel catalogue of violence. Maw vented his anger in the girls' direction, starting with Charlene.

"Just get out of here, you useless fucking bitch."

Charlene was not going to just soak up the abuse. The time had come. Her mother had put up with too much for too long.

"You're scum," she shouted back.

Maw visibly boiled with anger at that reply. He saw himself as the man of the household. And here was his own daughter calling him names.

For a split second he looked menacingly at both defiant girls standing before him.

"I am not going to take this," he screamed.

Punches rained down on the back of Charlene's head. She had become the first one to feel the full force of his temper.

Maw's eyes were twisted up as he concentrated on thumping her as hard as he could. Harder and harder. He kept crashing his massive fists down on her neck bone. He wanted to crush her body, bludgeon her spirit until it caved in.

Even though they had all been expecting it, it took them all slightly by surprise. He had done it so many

149

times before but on this occasion it seemed worse than ever.

He was delirious with anger.

Then Annette joined in.

She tried to jump on her father's back to stop him throwing his punches. It was an impossible task.

"Stop you bastard. Stop." The screaming was even louder than before. They were fighting back this time. They were not going to let him get away with it. They had soaked up enough punishment. Now it was their turn to attack.

Maw relaxed his vicious onslaught for a moment.

Regathering his energy before starting all over again.

Charlene now had the opportunity to grab her sister by the hand and run to the shelter of their bedroom. It had been the only place throughout their childhood where he had not dared to inflict punishment.

Now they prayed he would respect their sanctuary.

As they dashed through the house, Charlene could feel the throbbing on her injured neck. Behind them they heard the drunken insults of their father. He was coming after them. He wanted to finish them off for good.

It was like a scene from the worst type of horror movie. He was chasing them. Every moment getting closer and closer.

But this was real life.

As they scrambled up the stairs, Maw lunged at Annette's ankle. He held on tight. She felt herself lose balance. She could not control it. She was falling backwards into his vice-like grasp. Charlene grabbed her arm and a human tug of war was waged on the stairway.

Maw pulled with all his might. Suddenly he lost balance and his daughter aimed a sharp kick to his face. She was free momentarily. But the chase was still on.

The stair carpet came loose and he lost his footing as the girls looked behind them. They were relieved to have escaped his grasp but they knew he would still come after them.

Somehow, he regained his footing and climbed the stairs three at a time. His anger seemed to be giving him fresh impetus in the race to the bedroom.

As Charlene turned to slam the door shut, she felt his weight against the door, forcing it open again. She tried with all her might to keep closing it. But the sheer strength of her father was too much.

For a few desperate seconds they pulled and pushed the door each way until he finally burst through.

Now he was in their room. They both had their backs to the paint peeled walls. Terrified of what was about to happen.

"Dad. Let's talk about this." Charlene was trying to calm him down. A peaceful approach might work. He seemed to hesitate for a moment, responding to his daughter's appeal.

Maybe he could see how dreadful he had been?

Then an umbrella came crashing down towards his head.

Annette saw it now as all out war – and this was no time to start waving the white flag.

Just as as the brolly was about to hit dead centre on his crown, Maw grabbed at it and pulled it out of her grasp.

He was in control once more. He had the upper hand and now he was going to teach those daughters of his a lesson they would never forget.

Grabbing Annette by the wrist, he threw a volley of punches at her. Once again, he aimed at the back of the neck. A favourite spot for family battering.

Perhaps he knew the bruises would not show so clearly.

Then Mrs Maw appeared at the door. The sight of her husband trying to kill their eldest daughter had inspired her to stoop to his level. She was armed with a huge mirror – ready to use at the earliest opportunity.

She pulled him to the floor and smashed the mirror over his head. The pieces scattered around the room. Maw lay unconscious. The beast had been tamed for a short while.

The three women were drained. Even by their father's appalling standards this was the nearest to death any of them had ever come. For a few seconds none of them said anything as they walked downstairs to recover from their ordeal.

In the kitchen Annette broke the silence.

"Let's kill him before he kills us." She was shaking from shock. Mrs Maw felt the same way. She nodded in agreement. But Charlene was horrified.

"Don't be so bloody stupid. Let's just leave him where he is and call the police." She wanted justice, not bloody retribution.

The other two women stopped and thought for a second. They knew in their heart of hearts that Charlene was right, but events clouded their judgement. All they could think about were the beatings, the insults and the terror. Year in, year out at the hands of a sick monster who deserved no mercy. Now they had a chance to do something about it. A chance to avenge incidents like the time he threatened to gas his own children when they annoyed him.

"The Gestapo had it about right. I just wish I had been Himmler then I could have had you lot put down at birth."

Thomas Maw was no joker. He had looked menacingly into his children's eyes as they all sat down one meal time. He had meant it.

However terrible he had been though, murder, whatever the motives, was wrong. Pure and simple. They knew that. They should look at the situation objectively. Recognise the symptoms and deal with them.

But human emotions are not that easy to contain.

The police should have been called there and then. But something held them back. They wanted to deal with him in their own way. Turn the tables on him. Even if they did call the police, it required a real effort because they had no telephone. It made it more difficult to reach the obvious, sensible decision.

Nevertheless they had to decide what to do before he regained consciousness.

"Go next door and call the police. We've got to get him out of this house." Both Annette and her mother had come round and seen sense.

The temptation to take the law into their own hands had passed. It would have seemed "just" to cause him some pain – just as he had done to them for so long. But, underneath it all, they knew the police were the only answer. They could deal with him. Hopefully, the courts would put him away for a very long time.

Charlene was relieved. For a few desperate minutes she had seemed to be the only person in that house who wanted to take the correct course of action. The only way of dealing with a fascist is to become a fascist – unless sense prevails. Finally it had.

Charlene went to put on a coat. She had to hurry.

Upstairs, Maw was stirring.

A hand grabbed Annette around the throat. She hadn't seen it coming.

Maw was going to finish his private war with his own family. His wife and daughters might have decided to treat him like a human being, but he was not going to do them that service in return.

Annette was gasping for breath. He was smiling gleefully at his other daughter and her mother as he held Annette by the throat.

Maybe he had heard about their plans to murder him? Perhaps he had decided to kill them before they managed to do away with him? One thing was for certain. Maw was now trying his hardest to murder Annette.

"Get a knife." Annette was struggling to spit out the words but Charlene understood what she was saying.

She hesitated, still longing for a peaceful solution. Even as their father stood there trying to choke her sister to death, she hoped he would stop and they could sit down and discuss their problems, instead of turning that night into a life or death struggle.

Charlene hesitated… but she knew.

There was no time. She had to get the knife.

"For God's sake… He's killing me!"

Charlene ran to the kitchen and grabbed the nearest knife she could find. She could have picked the huge carving knife on the sideboard, but she chose the small cutlery knife instead.

Annette grabbed it from her and plunged it into Maw's body. She had to be quick. She might not live much longer…

As the blade sank into his stomach, Annette felt her father let go. She thought she had plunged it deep into his body but as he turned it just snapped in two. It did not even penetrate his outer layer of skin.

Now the monster had switched victims and was punching his wife viciously like a prize fighter desperate to gain an instant knock-out.

"A bigger one! Quick!" Annette screamed

Annette was trying desperately to stop her father from killing her mother. She punched him in the back, but it had little effect. It just drove him on to further violence. Charlene went back into the kitchen once more. This time she got the carving knife that would finish off the job.

Annette snatched the knife away from her younger sister like a heroin user grabbing at her fix. But she was more desperate than any drug addict. She had to kill him before he struck first.

She plunged the seven inch blade into his neck, severing the jugular vein in one quick motion. But he still kept punching, despite blood gushing from the wound all over his wife and daughter. So Annette continued to stab at the neck with all the strength she could muster. Within seconds the monster had crumpled in a heap on the floor.

At last the pain and suffering would be no more.

Annette and Charlene Maw were each jailed for three years when they admitted killing Thomas Maw, before a judge at Leeds Crown Court on Nov 17, 1980. They were originally charged with murder but this was reduced to manslaughter.

A later appeal against their sentence saw Charlene's term cut by six months. Annette's appeal was dismissed.

Charlene was said to have 'played a lesser part' in the killing, according to the appeal court judge, Lord Lane.

He said Annette was the probable organiser of the offence. At the time of their original sentencing, Judge Mr Justice Smith acknowledged that the sisters had been provoked and that their life was 'a sad history'. But he also added, "It is also a very sad duty I have to perform because you deliberately and unlawfully stabbed and killed him".

8

Death Wish: The mother who struck back

Lubeck is a town steeped in tradition. With a 15th Century gate and two plump towers, it is so typically German that it even figures on the fifty mark banknote.

The sheer greyness of the place is daunting when you first walk down its sterile streets.

Block upon block of tidy buildings, never more than ten storeys in height, set a severe backdrop against a population where few people smile and the emphasis is on survival rather than happiness.

On May 4, 1980 residents went about their business in a cold, almost fearful way. Rarely stopping to chat as they performed their chores for the day.

Provincial German towns nearly all share that slightly dead atmosphere in daytime. They only come alive when darkness has fallen and the nightlife takes over to become the life blood of virtually every man under the age of 60.

There is a commonly held theory about this stark contrast. The Germans work very hard to earn a living. That means they tend to play even harder.

A night on the town in Lubeck was usually a three stage affair for the typical middle-aged male resident, out with a couple of workmates.

Naturally, food would come first. And that could mean a massive three or even four course meal in one of the town's many restaurants. A dinner consisting of everything from *sauerkraut* to those huge fat sausages. All washed down with vast litre mugs of beer.

Then your typical group would wander to one of the livelier bars in Lubeck where they would regale each other with blustery tales of woe covering a range of topics from soccer to politics.

By about 9.30pm everyone would be well and truly on the way to drink-induced euphoria. This was when the insatiable appetite for sex took over.

They flock to the brothels that are always on the

outskirts of town. The townsfolk all know they exist, but they don't want to hear about them or see them. In Lubeck, the brothels attract far more sightseers than those plump twin towers.

Names like "The Fun Palace" and "The LA Club" were popular. The Germans have always felt more reassured by brothels with American sounding names. They like that familiar ring to them.

The set-up, though, was always exactly the same: the customers paid a nominal entrance fee. Then they would stroll up to the bar and order a drink. Suddenly, at least six girls, in outfits that usually consisted of skimpy basques, stockings and white stilettos, would appear as if by magic and start flirting outrageously.

For the uninitiated it was a most fulfilling experience because men on their first visit nearly always presumed these girls were only interested in them. They would frequently believe that their good looks and magnetic character had attracted all these single, unattached beauties to swarm around them, like bees in a honeypot. The fact the girls are virtually undressed seemed incidental at the time.

Anyway Marianne Bachmeier and her live-in lover Christian Berthold weren't complaining. They ran one of the most popular bars in Lubeck and it just happened to be the perfect stopping off point for many of those men who were planning an eventual visit to "The Fun Palace."

Marianne, aged 30, with long dark brown hair was a stunning looking woman, more than a capable match for the hundreds of leering, lecherous men who poured into her bar.

She worked in a soft, sensual yet efficient manner. Never offending the customers but at the same time sometimes flirting outrageously with men who caught her eye.

Marianne was a woman who had spent her whole life craving for love and attention. Her fanatical Nazi

157

father was soon replaced by a brutal step father who regularly gave her vicious beatings. She hated him so much she couldn't even bring herself to call him anything other than "Uncle Paul."

A vicious sex attack by a saleman left an even more indeliable mark on her childhood. She was just nine at the time. As she reached her mid–teens, Marianne blossomed into a beautiful young woman. She longed for someone to genuinely love her but far too many men wanted her for entirely the wrong reasons.

It was therefore no surprise that she ended up with Christian. After countless disastrous relationships, two brutal rapes and two pregnancies, Marianne was desperate for someone whose intentions were genuine. She had already worked up an unhealthy dislike and distrust of men. She needed to find someone who could restore her faith in the other sex.

Christian seemed to be a gentle hippy, only interested in love and peace, when the couple first met at an all-night party hosted by an oddball friend called "Yogi." Marianne was immediately taken by Christian – and slept with him within hours of that first meeting. They both felt a bond of friendship and love and soon moved in together.

Then she discovered he was a wealthy innkeeper and she actually had some money to spend for the first time in her life. That first bar was in Kiel. It was a great success. They were happy days for Marianne.

Christian sold the business for a fortune. They bought a floating gin palace. But that didn't do so well and that was how they ended up in Lubeck in yet another bar.

Meanwhile, Marianne and Christian's love for each other had turned into a roller coaster of emotional ups and downs. Each often sleeping with someone else as a cry for help when the relationship had seemed to be disolving.

Somehow they remained together and seven years previously, they had even had a child, Anna, as proof of their love, however tormented it might have been.

Now, here was Marianne playing mine perfect host inside the smokey, sweaty bar. Even though she always wore an apron over a sweater or blouse and sexy tight jeans, Marianne still managed to ooze a sensuous appeal – something that some people are born with while others are not.

Just 200 yards away, balding former butcher Klaus Grabowski was definitely not going to join the mass of Lubeck men out on a night of drink and vice.

He was a desperately shy man in his thirties. Sometimes he was so afraid to meet people that he would stay locked up in his tiny one-bedroomed flat in one of those grey town apartment buildings, fearful of the consequences if he should dare to venture out onto the streets.

His fiance was constantly on at him about his anti-social behaviour. "You cannot stay cooped up here all your life. You must get out. You have to meet people," she would tell him. As a result he only saw her once a week. They barely kissed each time they met. She longed to stay the night and make love with him but the urge on Grabowski's part was not there. She never forgot the night she stripped off all her clothing and tried to seduce him. He didn't even get sexually excited. She fled the flat without even bothering to put back on the red tights she had bought especially for the occasion. But she grew to believe this was all a sign of how honourable his intentions towards her really were. But she got sexual urges. How come he didn't? She wondered. They had been engaged to marry for seven years.

She simply had no idea what happened whenever Grabowski did encounter other people in one to one situations ...especially young people.

He had been a popular figure at his corner butcher's shop. There, he had had his regular customers. They all called him Herr Grabowski and treated him as a man of substance. They saw him as a fine butcher whose meat was second to none. They did not see beneath the heavy bearded face that gave him a Rasputin-like appearance. He was just your friendly, rounded butcher, always eager to please.

But that was all in the past. Grabowski had lost his job and his pride with it. He was a broken man who felt degraded by his non status in society.

Grabowski was preparing for bed. He had consumed two bottles of beer and he knew what would happen if he drunk. Those twinges would reawaken the devil that lurked within him. The evil thoughts that most men – according to Marianne Bachmeier – were constantly absorbed by. The intent was always there. It never actually went away for long...

Back at the bar Marianne too was desperate. She was worn out by the long hours she worked. Always on her feet, it was a gruelling profession. Constantly smiling at the customers, in response to their sexist, rude remarks. Wanting revenge when a drunken man tried to grab her breasts or another beast hung around until the bar emptied because he thought she would be an easy lay.

Luckily, Marianne, Christian and little Anna lived above the bar. At least she could avoid those creepy walks home she had endured when they ran the place in Kiel.

It always bugged her that they had agreed to split the responsibilites of running the bar. He insisted it was more sensible for them to take it in turns to manage the place rather than run it together and both end up working an eighty hour week.

The problem was that it meant they hardly saw each other. One was sleeping while the other was working. It was a recipe for disaster and Marianne knew it. But Christian was not the sleepy laid back hippy he once was. He had become a jaded, money-conscious businessman desperate for financial success. He felt all the pressures of the world on his shoulders. He became more and more pre-occupied with all his own problems. Giving Marianne and his family less and less attention. It marked the beginnings of a classic relationship breakdown.

The consequences of this attitude were clear for everyone to see. Marianne began to sleep with other people. Her craving for a long lasting genuine love had returned.

Christian was deeply hurt by her indiscretions and took his own sad revenge. He started visiting brothels – the temptations were all so close by.

On one occasion they hurt each other so badly that it was a miracle they managed to stick together. Marianne took it upon herself to travel to Hanover and search out an old boyfriend – the father of her second child, who had eventually been adopted. She tracked him down, but his reaction was to drive her into the countryside, rape her and leave her on a grass verge to find her own way home.

When Marianne arrived back at Christian's bar she poured the entire incident out to him. He was stunned. He had a feeling of anger at the man and betrayal by Marianne for bothering to locate him in the first place. But his emotions came out in the form of severe depression. They began rowing more and more.

One night, he stormed out of the flat and headed for his old haunts in Berlin. Unable to find any of his previous girlfriends, Christian visited one of the city's most notorious brothels.

He had sex for just 50 marks. But the cost to his relationship with Marianne was far higher. On his return to Lubeck, he described the entire experience to her. Every detail about the sex. The way he performed. The way the girl reacted. It was all too much for Marianne. Yet again she had been betrayed. Why did men treat her so badly? What was it in her character that prompted such punishment?

Marianne could not begin to answer those questions, so she did what many victims – especially women – see as the only solution. She retaliated in the most graphic, hurtful way.

"Let's see how he will react if I become the whore," she thought to herself. "Will he still want me after that? I want to make him realise how dirty and heartless it is to sell your body. He'll soon find out what it is like to live with a prostitute."

Just a few hours later, Marianne was walking the streets of Berlin herself, waiting for the first man to come along so she could sell her body to him. She found a man and instantly hated herself for it. But, in her eyes, it just had to be done. It was her own special brand of punishment for the man she longed to continue loving.

Somehow, through all this bruising tit-for-tat behaviour, Christian and Marianne continued to survive, although their friends believed it was now only a matter of time until they split.

On May 4, 1980, Little Anna she slept blissfully in her bed in the flat above the bar – unaware of the torment and guilt that constantly enveloped her parents' lives.

As Klaus Grabowski prepared for his own bed that evening, he heard the din of the music coming from the bar. It was 11pm and a couple of drunks were stumbling up the road outside his flat still dreaming of the sex they would like to enjoy with that beautiful barmaid Marianne.

Women like that were the farthest thing from Grabowski's mind. His fantasies were far more obscure. They delved the depths of degradation.

His recurring thoughts concerned the sort of sex that would horrify those friendly housewives who'd always made such polite conversation with him at the butcher's shop. No doubt those customers would have grabbed one of those huge, razor sharp meat knives and turned on him if they had even vaguely realised what fantasies flowed consistently through his mind.

As he lay there in his bed, Grabowski conjured up pictures of what he wanted to do. The pain and suffering he wanted to inflict. The screams of fear. The cries of horror. The look on their faces when he fulfilled his sick desires. All the time his face would freeze in an ever-so-slight smile as he came closer and closer to reaching the climax he so longed to get to but knew he could not attain.

Even by his own sordid standards, this particular fantasy was vivid and life like. Grabowski felt as if he were actually there, doing it. He imagined in a frenzy the agony he was causing. And he wanted more and more.

This was a dream he did not want to escape from. He didn't want to leave. He wanted it to go on and on and on. Each time he saw her face, it drove him wild.

The fact that he was thinking up atrocities of such ferocity and brutality that they would be entirely unacceptable in any society did not seem to matter. Grabowski had long since given up any respect for human decency. His life was going nowhere. He had to have something to cling on to. Realizing just one those fantasies was his ultimate aim...

Marianne was cleaning up the last few glasses after a heavy night. It was almost one a.m. and she was virtually asleep on her feet. Just a few minutes earlier she had pushed the last letching hanger-on out of the front door and started performing the most tedious duty of every evening in the bar – straightening out the premises before retiring for bed.

Christian had decreed that no matter how tired either of them felt, the place had to be spotless for the next day. Marianne knew he was right but on this night she was feeling particularly tired.

Anna had not been sleeping well and it was a

strenuous existence. Marianne constantly had to get up early with Anna to prepare her for school at seven am. It was often only a few hours after she had gone to sleep.

The past few days had been even worse than usual. Marianne was so tired she had failed on two out of the five previous school days to wake up in time to pack Anna off to classes.

The seven-year-old was delighted. Missing school was a treat. Marianne was worried. She didn't want to end up losing Anna. She was so special to her. She had kept Marianne's life together. Without Anna, her life would fall apart again. She was painfully aware of that fact.

Marianne had given birth to two children before Anna. Both of them were now in care. A pregnancy at sixteen and an unhappy relationship had cost her those children. Anna represented her last chance to prove she was a capable mother. She loved her dearly and that constant threat made her even more special in Marianne's eyes.

Anna was a bubbly bright little girl, street-wise well beyond her years. Everyone liked her. She had a charming, elf-like face with well cut blonde hair. The relatives were convinced she could easily become a model in later years.

She also shared a unique bond of friendship with her mother. They were more like sisters than mother and daughter. Marianne would turn to Anna and vice versa. It was a remarkably close relationship. Some said too close.

But not only did Anna share her entire life with Marianne, she also shared her mother's personality in one, very significant way. Anna had magnetic qualities that attracted people – all sorts of people. Her mother had always longed for love and attention. It came out in a semi-flirtatious sort of way. But it had also led to that incident with the saleman that scarred her for life. She had been just nine–years–old at the time. Marianne just prayed and hoped that nothing similar would happen to her daughter. But she

164

constantly feared the worse. There were always bastards around to prey on the innocent and vulnerable.

By the time Marianne finally fell into bed in the apartment above the bar that night, she was feeling shattered. It had been a hell of a long day.

In the bedroom just a few feet away, Anna slept soundly for once. Completely unaware of what was to come.

Next morning, there was an air of panic in Marianne's household. It was nine a.m. and Anna had not risen in time for school. Christian was only concerned with one thing – the bar. He had to be downstairs to manage the beer deliveries due at any moment. He was furious because Anna was going to miss another day of school. With Marianne's previous problems, they could ill-afford to get a visit from the social welfare people. They would soon misinterpret Anna's recent non-appearances in class.

To make matters worse still, Marianne had an appointment in the centre of town. It was a private thing. She didn't want to discuss it with anyone. Whatever the appointment was, she could not take Anna with her. Marianne was a secretive person at times. It was, no doubt, something to do with her childhood. She would often bottle up her innermost thoughts. Sometimes that could put her under enormous pressure, not to mention the people around her.

It was a private appointment and she had to get there by ten at the latest. She would say no more.

The only person not panicking was Anna. She was looking forward to a day off school.

Marianne was angry with Christian. She had told him she had this appointment. Why didn't he stay behind? They continued arguing. It all seemed perfectly normal to the little seven-year-old.

If they had leaned out of the window of the living room that morning, they all would have seen Klaus

165

Grabowski making his way up the street to go shopping.

He was cycling along the street in quite a rush to make it to the shops before opening time.

Grabowski was well known to his neighbours he might have been fired from his job after a recent prison term but he was still known as the butcher to many locals. But – without exception – they had only seen one side of his character. Certainly they regularly spoke with him. But only to comment on the weather or the price of meat. Never on a personal level. Never prying into his strange mind.

With those cold steely grey eyes perhaps many of them would rather not know. It was this very fact that enabled Klaus to continue living in his sick fantasy world where reality only occasionally interrupted proceedings. It gave him the smoke screen to indulge his evil thoughts. Even his fiancé asked few questions. She just accepted he was a shy, frightened man who needed gentle coaxing not difficult questions that might make him face up to his own inadequacies. That was probably why they only saw each other once a week.

By the time Klaus got to the bread shop a queue had already formed. All the housewives there that morning knew Grabowski. They were grateful for a new face to talk to as they waited. But their children weren't so keen. There was something about him that used to scare a lot of them. In the butcher's shop, they were always catching a glance from him and turning away shyly even when he offered them a sweet from behind the counter.

He had this strange glint in his eye. It used to sparkle flatly when he spotted a mother and her children queueing in the shop. For a moment his eyes would stray to those of one of the children... just as he chopped those pieces of tender sirloin into managable pieces. Then they would dart around the faces of everyone inside the shop. Sizing them up as he lunged at his carcases with that huge knife. Some mothers used to wonder how he could cut everything so perfectly when he was looking away from it.

At the flat above the bar, Marianne was rushing out
of the front door. As she kissed Anna on the forehead,
she told her to behave herself and not to go out of
the apartment; an invitation to an inquisitive child, if
ever there was one.

Marianne rushed down the stairs to catch a bus she
had spotted from the living room window. She did not
really have time to think about why she was leaving
a seven-year-old girl alone in the home to fend for
herself. She had too many other problems on her mind.

Her relationship with Christian was crumbling one
moment and passionate the next. She knew it was only
a matter of time before they would break up.

Anna, on the other hand, was looking forward to doing
exactly what she wanted for a whole day. She was a free
spirit with an enquiring mind. She wanted to explore.

After all, this wasn't the first time that she had been
left to fend for herself. On the last occasion, she and
her best friend Maria had been alone on the streets
near their home for hours. And they'd had a great
adventure. They met two really nice cats and were
invited into an apartment by their owner to help feed
them. It had been really fun.

Anna had no pets of her own and, like any young
child, she longed to give love and affection to a dog
or a cat or some sort of animal. As she and Maria
gently stroked the two tabbies they felt tempted to pick
them up and take them home. Then their nice owner
had appeared and offered them a chance to feed them.

The two little girls did not hesitate to go back to
the man's apartment – all those warnings from their
mothers had fallen on deaf ears. Their thoughts were
dominated by their affection for these two cats – not
the evil intentions of the outside world.

Their naive faith in mankind was still intact. They
had not been through the trials and torment suffered
by their parents.

Anna and Maria had no need to fear as long as they stuck together. For even the sickest people rarely want their atrocities to be witnessed by anyone else. Their intentions are so degrading that they find it uncomfortable if anyone else is present, whatever their age.

They knew their parents would be angry if they said what they had done, so they promised each other not to tell anyone about their adventure.

But, on this day, Anna was on her own. Maria was at school and Anna needed to find something to do. As she looked out of the window the answer to the problem seemed to be cycling slowly up the street.

As Anna skipped down the stairs to catch up with the friend she had just seen, she just kept thinking about those two sweet little cats. How she wished she had some of her own. Then, on those days when she was left alone, she would not seem so lonely.

On the sidewalk, she soon caught up with her friend. Anna never actually knew his name but that didn't matter. She was more interested in the cats than him.

Klaus Grabowski's eyes glinted the moment he felt the little hand tugging at his sleeve from behind. He instantly recognised Anna from her visit with Maria to his flat some weeks earlier.

He quickly glanced around him to see if anyone had noticed their encounter. No one seemed to be taking the slightest bit of notice. He was hardly able to contain himself. Here was the little girl he was so especially fond of. The little girl who seemed so incredibly attractive. The one he had dreamed about...

A few minutes later, at his apartment, he was positively shaking with lurid excitement. Here she was. The one he had earmarked. The little girl he wanted.

Anna was stroking the cat, showing the sort of affection Grabowski had longed for as a child but never received.

He was running out of patience. He had got her to his apartment. Now he wanted only one thing.

Only a few hours earlier he had fantasised about the

sexual perversity that gave him his only thoughts of pleasure. Now he had a disgusting opportunity to achieve it. Nothing was going to stop him.

Anna was crying now. She did not like the "game" that Grabowski had insisted on playing. She wanted to go home but he wouldn't let her.

He hated the crying. He wanted to stop it – *now*. He couldn't stand the noise. It was making him feel vulnerable. But he had to go on punishing her, hurting her. It was wrong but he did not care. He just had to have his way. No grown woman would tolerate such behaviour. This was why he had to have them so young. He hated the way women had always dominated his life. He wanted to punish them for existing. This was his way of getting his own back.

Anna was screaming hysterically now. She knew that this should not be happening. She knew this man was evil. She knew she had to get out of that apartment. But there was no way she could break free. He had a vice like grip on her. Then she fainted.

Grabowski felt the pulse. She hadn't died yet. He went into the bedroom and pulled out a pair of his fiance's red tights from a drawer.

He used them to strangle the last drop of life out of this poor little innocent child.

Marianne had returned to her apartment. It was lunchtime. There was no sign of Anna. At first she didn't panic. Convinced that she had probably gone around to a friend's home.

One hour later, Marianne telephoned the police in a distressed state. All the memories of her own awful childhood were flooding back. She just kept thinking about that salesman who assaulted her. The horrible stepfather. The neighbour who raped her. It was a terrible world out there. She knew, because all her life she had been a victim.

She could feel that something was terribly wrong. She did not want to think what might have happened.

But, inside herself she knew...

Grabowski was still in a sexual trance. He had the lifeless body of little Anna in his arms and he was placing the corpse into a cardboard box that he had in the kitchen of his cramped apartment.

He didn't flinch as he crumpled the tiny body into the three foot square box. For a man who had thrown the carcases of animals around for a living this was hardly difficult.

It was now late in the afternoon and he needed to dispose of Anna's body quickly and secretly. But Grabowski had one problem – transport. He did not own a car – just a tatty bicycle. He was going to have to use it to carry her body.

Clinically, as if he was carrying a hefty Christmas present, he strapped the box onto the front of the bike and began to ride. At first, the sheer weight made him slightly unsteady. But, as he gained speed, his balance returned. For half an hour he cycled towards the outskirts of the town, contantly looking for the perfect site for a grave.

Grabowski began digging a shallow hole with the shovel he had tied to the back of his bicycle.

He was shaking with fear by now. The reality of the situation was slowly catching up with him and he was beginning to realise what he had done.

As he gently dropped the cardboard box into the ground, he could feel the weight of the body slipping over to one side making it difficult to balance. It must have finally drove home to him the enormity of what he had just done.

He thought for a moment about the lives he had wrecked beyond repair. How one sick moment of sexual satisfaction would ruin so many people's futures. Not to mention the future of Anna Bachmeier.

Grabowski was now suffering the pangs of guilt that should have been there from the beginning. As he cycled back to his flat, he found it impossible to stop his mind wandering back to the look on the face of little Anna as she tried in vain to fight back.

He kept asking himself the same question over and over again. Why? Why? Why? Something deep inside him made his conscience actually prick. The tragedy was that he did not feel it before. Then perhaps Anna would have lived a full life.

Grabowski drove directly to the town's main police station and confessed to his crime.

It was an unusually warm day in Lubeck on Friday, March 6, 1981.

In the tiny courtroom where Klaus Grabowski was on trial for the murder of little Anna Bachmeier, the atmosphere was relaxed.

Outside, the sun was shining. Inside, the defendant had already admitted his guilt. The public gallery was empty except for a group of school children studying German law.

There were few press members covering the event. After all, this was just another in a long catalogue of sex crimes against young children – it was too common-place to make headline news.

The only person – apart from the judge and the lawyers – remotely interested in the sad proceedings was Marianne Bachmeier. She sat at a table just ten feet from the defendant watching his every response.

There was no dock for this monster. Under German law a defendant is allowed to sit at a table like everyone else – until he is found guilty. Even though Grabowski had already confessed to his atrocities.

By Marianne stood a four inch high, framed photograph of the daughter he had butchered. Every few seconds she would look at his face and then down at the face of her pretty little Anna. She had behaved in exactly the same way throughout the trial – which was now into its third day.

Marianne had looked glazed much of the time but it was clear she was listening intently to every awful detail of her daughter's horrible death and the background of the man who had murdered her.

Klaus Grabowski had lived in and around the Lubeck area for most of his rather sad, pathetic life. In the early 1970s he had been twice convicted for the sexual abuse of children. On both occasions he had lured innocent little girls into his home and brutally assaulted them leaving them psychologically and physically scarred for life.

While serving his sentence, Grabowski had himself been sexually abused and beaten up by fellow prisoners.

Traditionally, child sex offenders are the most hated inhabitants inside prison. Wardens would turn their heads the other way, whenever Grabowski found himself facing an angry mob.

By 1976, he was desperate to get out of jail. The beatings were proving unbearable and he knew that no-one would help him. After all, he was a pervert and a threat society.

Then Grabowski volunteered to be castrated to secure an early release from prison. It was his only chance. In a short operation, he permitted his sexual urges to be destroyed for ever – or so all the experts had believed.

To lose his manhood seemed a small price to pay for the escape from the daily abuse of his fellow prisoners. But life on the outside proved tough for Grabowski. He never got his old job back as a butcher and his world seemed hopeless. He wanted to find someone to love but there was no love within. The old, sick urges seemed to have subsided. But he wanted more out of life.

Grabowski had no sexual feelings whatsoever, but he was fully aware what they felt like because he had once had them. Now his life would be empty forever – unless he could plan a way to get those responses back.

The answer lay in hormone treatment. The very thought of those sexual feelings returning motivated him to seek help.

In 1979, just a few months before he made helpless Anna his victim, Grabowski tricked his way into getting help from a urologist. He perusaded the medic to give him the neccessary hormone treatment to help him get those deadly urges back.

172

He did not admit that he had been castrated because of the sex offences he had committed. Instead he persuaded the doctor to help on the grounds that he was simply an exhibitionist.

But now, he assured the physician, he was cured and he wanted his sex life back. The doctor didn't bother to check his record.

On the day he murdered Anna, Grabowski's hormone levels were as high as that of a normal man.

Marianne listened to all this evidence impassively. She was stunned by revelation after revelation but she had no right in a court of law to stand up and air her opinions. She had to bottle up her feelings of anger, disgust and sadness. Being repressed had long since become a way of life for Marianne.

And then there was the guilt. How could she have left her daughter alone? Why didn't she just take her with her into town? If only she could turn the clock back. But it was too late.

All this was a dreadful repetition of her own tragic life. She had so desperately hoped things would turn out differently for Anna.

Her best friend, pretty blonde lawyer Brigitte Muller-Horn recalled how: "Anna's death was more important to her than her own death. In a way, she died with Anna. Anna was a very bright and clever child. More like a small adult than a little girl. She was her mother's confidante and friend. Marianne talked to Anna about problems like she could talk to no one else. She was closer to her than she had ever been to anyone else in her entire life."

All these thoughts and much more were rushed through Marianne's mind as she continued her court room vigil.

Just one hour earlier, Marianne had visited her daughter's grave in the vast; impersonal cemetery in the centre of Lubeck. She had kneeled at the tiny white cross and begged forgiveness. She felt the weight of guilt about Anna's death. There were so many ifs.

If only she had not gone out to that appointment. If only they had never sold the bar in Kiel. If only she had woken up on time to send Anna to school. The list was endless.

Back in the court Grabowski was centre stage.

Marianne looked into straight into his cold, almost dead eyes but he turned away. Now her mind returned to the murder scene.

"He had his hands around her throat. I heard her scream..."

At that moment Marianne fumbled under the green coat on her lap. She pulled out a small Beretta pistol, aimed at Grabowski's back and squeezed the trigger six times.

She watched coldly as his body jerked from the hail of bullets that hit him. No one could do anything to help the former butcher as he slumped to the floor. He died instantly.

She then calmly threw the gun aside, sending it skidding across the floor of the stunned court room. Marianne stood up to allow police to escort her from the building.

When she visited Lubeck Cemetry to select Anna's last resting place, the undertaker asked her: "Would you like to select a single or a double grave?"

Without hesitation, Marianne replied: "A double. It is for Anna and me. Soon I will be with her anyway."

Marianne had chosen the courts of justice, to exact an ancient retribution: an eye for an eye.

She had avenged her daughter's death in a fashion that no-one in the entire world could fail to sympathise with.

In March, 1983, Marianne Bachmeier was sentenced to six years imprisonment after being found guilty of the murder of Klaus Grabowski. Immediately after her sentence was pronounced she was allowed free, pending an appeal, after which her sentence was reduced to two years suspended. She is now happily re-married and living in a cottage on the Baltic coast.

9

Blind Rage

Her hair was thick, lustrous and so dark it might have been spun on the same loom as the night. Her shoulders and back were slender. Her legs were turned to one side, covered up to mid-thigh by sheer black stockings. The curve of her calves was distinct and, under different circumstances, might well have been considered sexually appealing.

The shapely legs, the full hips, the trim waist, the full breasts – all were fully exposed. But it was her face that gave it all away.

The matt grey eyes stared blankly into the moonlight. The rain pelted on to her face then ran down her breasts, exposed by the ripped open blue nurse's uniform that partially covered her lillywhite body. Her pubic hair was soaked by the rain, her underwear long since removed. At the back of her head was a small hole rimmed with a black burn mark – the only evidence of assault.

There was no-one else at Broat's Farm. Just a corpse in the muddy yard as the rain slammed hard against the ground on that bitterly cold December evening.

The body of nurse Jayne Smith lay there uncovered. It was an undignified death for anyone. The apparent victim of an horrific sexual assault. Something that no woman could ever wish on her worst enemy.

A tiny beam of light from the farmhouse illuminated the lower half of the corpse, highlighting the tops of her thighs and glistening against her drenched stockings.

The whole scene seemed staged. As if some movie director would emerge from the shadows and shout "Cut" so the actress could get up and walk back to her trailer for a fresh application of make-up. But the body did not stir. And the film crew never materialised.

A car came around the corner into the entrance to the farm. As the headlights panned across the yard, they momentarily picked out the body. The car jerked to a sudden halt. The driver scrambled out, leaving the door swinging on its hinges, and slid through the muddy yard to the crumpled body of Jayne Smith.

Before he even reached her body, William Smith knew she was dead. There was no movement. The body was twisted slightly out of shape. His wife of just seven months lay, lifeless, in front of him. For a few moments, he just blinked. Unable to absorb the awfulness of what had happened. He squeezed his eyes tightly shut in the hope that when he opened them again, she would be gone – back inside their farmhouse, making him supper lovingly. Smiling at him lovingly. Being a good wife lovingly.

She was still there. Abused and dead.

William knelt in the puddle beside her body, immune to the icy wind that swept up from the North Yorkshire moors. He took her hand in his. Desperate for one last response before she was taken from him for ever.

He felt her fingers. The nails. The softness of the skin that had been so very much alive just a few hours before.

He squeezed her hand tightly. The cold clamminess did not matter. At least he was here. With her. Showing how much he really loved and cared for her.

He moved his hand further down into her palm, pressing tight. Something was missing. But in the emotional turmoil that had occured during the past few minutes, he could not make out what it was.

He moved his hand up towards her fingers once more. Despite the tears that welled up in his eyes and throbbing pain of tension in his head, he kept feeling her hand. Why this? He had to know. He had to know.

He looked down at the limp discoloured fingers. And he realized with a jolt what was missing.

Her wedding ring.

Somehow his numb fingers punched in the three numbers.

"You've got to help me."

After a few seconds, a WPC came on the line. She sensed it immediately. She could tell that this was genuine.

"My wife has been murdered at home. I have just got in."

His voice was straining all the time. It was almost impossible to say that word. *Murdered*. It thumped the truth home to him.

He wasn't sure if he could continue with the call. What was the point? Nothing was going to bring Jayne back. No amount of sympathy. No miracle cure. She had gone forever.

William was a pragmatic man. As a child, he had always been taught to bottle up his emotions and never cry in public. "Men don't do that sort of thing son," his father once told him. But now he wanted to shed floods of tears. Let his emotions loose on the phone to a complete stranger. What would his folks have said to that?

He had to continue. He took a deep breath.

"She's laid in the yard. There is blood all over."

Blood. Just one word. It was there. It was real. His voice was really choking now. He just didn't know if he could go through with it.

She was dead. There was no future without her. How could he carry on?

Another deep breath gave him just enough courage.

"Her clothes have been removed and she looks as though she has been raped and murdered."

He slammed the phone down after spitting out the words. It was the first contact he had had with anyone since the discovery. Now he knew it really was actually happenning. The nightmare had begun.

Yet just seven months earlier, this dreadful episode wouldn't have seemed possible to twenty-eight-year-old Jayne Wilford and farmer William Smith, seven years her senior.

177

Their wedding had been beautiful. Held at a church in the heart of the North Yorkshire Moors, it had seemed like a scene out of Wuthering Heights. Farmers and their families gathered for a really happy occasion in a picturesque setting.

Although it was May, 1988, it could easily have been any time this century. Time does not seem to catch up with anything in that part of the world. Relatives and friends were convinced the happy couple would be together till they died. They had that feeling about them.

They seemed to go so well together.

William, a shy, bearded, hard working man of the land. Jayne, the caring, outgoing nurse who looked forward to having a family by the man she first fell for when she was still at school.

They say opposites attract each other to make the perfect marriages. In their case, it looked like being true.

Yet it could all have been so very different for William.

Just over a year earlier, he had been due to marry another, older woman when Jayne stepped back into his life.

Yvonne Sleightholme had wanted William from the first moment she clapped eyes on him, at a rugby club disco on New Year's Eve, 1979. Beneath her rather staid clothes and practical hairstyle, lurked a ruthlessly determined woman.

William had always been a bit of a slow starter, so she had to make the running in every sense of the word.

At first, William was happy to be led by Yvonne. She was a brittle, strong Yorkshire lass. Always planning every moment they had together. Nothing was too much for Yvonne. She enjoyed running his life for him.

It meant she could take control. She decided who they did and did not see. Which of his friends were in and which were out.

Yvonne had big plans for them. Including marriage.

178

William didn't even think about it at first. His world stopped at the gates to Broat's Farm. He just let her carry on with the arrangements. He kept meaning to take a step back and consider it all, but it was a busy time on the farm and he never got the chance. He just wanted a peaceful life. Married or not. It didn't make a whole lot of difference to him.

After eighteen months of courtship, he did not mind the idea of a wedding. He was approaching his thirties. Most people in those parts took the plunge by then.

Gradually, however, it dawned on him that marriage to Yvonne might not be such a good idea. She was brilliant at running his life. But surely there had to be more to love than just that? True, she had moved into his farm and it was nice to have a woman around. But marriage?

He took her out one day and quietly, but tactfully, told her it was over between them.

She was stunned. She had been about to book the wedding arrangements. How could he turn around and dump her without any warning? There wasn't even anyone else.

Regular churchgoer Yvonne saw in William someone she genuinely felt she could love and cherish for the rest of her life. Someone who was soft, gentle and considerate. Someone completely malleable. She was not going to let him go that easily.

A few weeks later, she insisted they meet for one last time.

William agreed because he did not want to hurt her feelings. He soon began to wish he hadn't.

"I've got leukaemia – and it's all your fault." Yvonne was shouting, close to tears, at William. "It's got worse since you finished with me. You've got to do something."

William was speechless. Here was the woman he had cleanly and kindly tried to finish a relationship with, insisting that he had sentenced her to death by not continuing their affair.

He didn't expect a lot out of life. But why was she saying these things? It wasn't his fault, surely? But William was a trusting sort of bloke and Yvonne Sleightholme convinced him it was all his fault. Riddled with guilt, he agreed to carry on their courtship. He could not bear to see anyone so ill. Perhaps there was a chance she might recover now, he thought.

Miraculously, all traces of the illness disappeared within weeks of them getting back together. And William even began to think that maybe they did belong to each other. Perhaps fate had meant them to get together again? She was a good woman after all.

So William was hardly surprised when Yvonne began making new arrangements for a wedding.

This time, she told herself, he won't get away.

"I want this wedding," she said. "It is going to happen. It is going to be the most beautiful day of my life."

Yvonne was in her element. Being a doctor's receptionist was clearly taking second place to her latest career – organising her forthcoming marriage.

The date was set six months ahead to give her ample time to sort out the church, the dress, the reception, the honeymoon. It was all very time consuming and Yvonne did so love to organise...

Meanwhile, William carried on working hard at the farm, rarely having time to go out except to attend the countless fittings for his morning suit and to see the vicar to discuss the ceremony.

On one rare, fateful trip into the nearby town of Salton, he bumped into his old friend Jayne Wilford.

They had once been very close. But both had drifted off into different directions after she had reached her twenties. William often thought about what had happened to Jayne. But she always seemed to have a new boyfriend on her arm whenever he saw her. She seemed to have outgrown him or so he presumed.

Jayne had heard about the wedding plans and wanted to give him her congratulations. There was, of course, another motive for seeking him out. She also thought a lot about William.

"You know. I always reckoned that one day we would get married. It has always been one of my secret dreams."

William was shocked but at the same time, pleased. It was exactly what he hoped she would say. There had always been something special between them. They might have drifted apart years before, but there was always a feeling that destiny might play a hand in bringing them together once more.

Jayne wasn't just trying to steal another woman's husband-to-be. She had a chilling message to deliver to the man she really loved more than anyone else.

"I think you are being conned into a relationship that you know is not right for you."

William listened intently. In the back of his mind these were the very things he feared about his impending marriage to Yvonne.

Jayne went on, "You are being dragged into a relationship by someone who is lying and scheming."

William nodded his head in agreement. He knew that every word she was saying was true. Yet how could he break off his relationship with Yvonne? He was well aware of the hurt he would cause.

For a few weeks, William was in a complete quandry. Every time he started to tell Yvonne that it was off, she would over-ride the conversation with her prattle about the arrangements for the wedding.

William then did something he had never contemplated ever doing in his life. He slept with both Jayne and Yvonne at the same time. He was unable to break the news to Yvonne. It was a remarkable sham. And he hated himself for it. It tormented him.

Betrayal did not come easily to William. Some men cheat all their lives, but William had never done it. Now the strain of keeping up a relationship with two women at the same time was tearing him apart emotionally. He could not stand it. He knew it was wrong. And it was impossible to know if Yvonne realised. She just seemed so wrapped up in those damned wedding arangements.

Yvonne's family were delighted their daughter had at last found happiness. She had lived at home on their farm for so long they had been worried she might remain a spinster for life. William seemed *such* a lovely character.

It was all yet more pressure on him. Making it more and more difficult to come clean. Yvonne had long since moved into his farm, making herself busy putting her own inimitable female stamp on the decor. Choosing new curtains, kitchen equipment and other essentials that had always been missing when William lived there alone.

He was guilty of cowardice and he knew it. By letting her continue to think he was willing to marry, he was just getting deeper and deeper into trouble.

Jayne kept urging him. Aware of what it must be like for the other woman. She was just as uncomfortable with this blatant deception. She kept thinking how she would have felt if the situations were reversed.

Then it happened. The one thing no-one ever plans for, but everyone dreads just before a wedding. Yvonne became pregnant. She became distraught because she might not fit into the wedding dress. For days she told no-one her secret. Fearful of the shame it might bring on them, but especially worried about that dress. In North Yorkshire, they still frowned upon children conceived outside marriage.

All the tension had tragic consequences because, within a few days, she had miscarried. No-one knew about the baby except her doctor.

Meanwhile, William was wracked with guilt about his affair with Jayne. He decided he had to tell her the truth.

"I've found someone else. I just don't think it would be right to carry on. Let's finish it for good this time."

He was trying to be honourable. He had confessed

his deception and now he just wanted them to finish peacefully. He knew he had done wrong. But he was coming clean. Telling the truth was the only way he knew. He felt it had gone on for quite long enough.

Yvonne was devastated. The hurt was immeasurable. She was still in love with him. She was just weeks from marrying him. What could she tell their relatives and friends?

But, perhaps worse of all, she had just lost his baby – and he hadn't even known she was pregnant. She needed his love and support through her difficult time. She didn't want to hear that the man she was about to marry had fallen in love with another woman.

"I have just miscarried our baby."

William didn't know what to do. This was turning into an even more difficult situation. After her last attempt to keep him through lies, he didn't even know if she were telling the truth.

He felt awful, but no amount of sympathy would bring them back together yet again. He still couldn't marry her.

"I no longer have any desire for you. Don't you understand?"

It was hurting William almost as much as it was hurting her. But it had to be said.

"We have both tried so hard but it hasn't worked out. I want to be free to find out how I truly feel about Jayne."

William's words were so carefully put – even at such a crucial moment. Yvonne knew she could do nothing but accept that it was over, though underneath the polite, civilised conversation, she was nurturing a resentment and hatred that would bring horrific consequences.

Just a few months later Jayne Milford moved into Broat's Farm.

The ghost of Yvonne Sleightholme had not yet been finally laid to rest. Unable to accept that it was completely over, she hadn't removed any of her belongings at first. It was as if she was convinced that William and Jayne would part and she could just carry on where she left off.

When she did eventually turn up, three months later, to gather her things, the atmosphere was strained and difficult. The three of them hardly uttered a word.

She soon left. Drove away from the farm, out of their lives forever. They hoped.

The voice at the other end of the phone line was menacing and cold.

"I'm going to kill you bitch..."

There was a click and the line went dead.

Jayne Smith had just returned with new husband William after their honeymoon.

Everyone gets cranky calls some times. But the voice seemed familiar.

No. It couldn't be her, thought Jayne. It was all over long ago. No-one could harbour such intense resentment surely? When she told William, he dismissed it in much the same way. The Smiths were a happy, trusting couple. They didn't really see the bad side of anyone. They didn't want to.

"Quick. Quick. There's a fire in the barn."

William rushed out into the yard. For almost half-an-hour he bravely dampened down the blaze with water and blankets.

It could have turned into a major catastrophe.

Strange really. He could not work out how on earth it had happened. Then he started to think that maybe it had been started deliberately. Perhaps *she* was responsible. Then again, no-one would go to those lengths. Would they?

"This is it. I've bloody well had enough of this nonsense. I'm going to see the police."

It was not often that William Smith lost his temper. But this time she had gone too far.

184

In his hand he held a wreath with a chilling message, "Jayne. I'll always remember you."

William was outraged.

"She's sick in the head. She's got to be stopped."

Domestic disputes don't come high on the police's list of priorities. Nevertheless, under pressure, they agreed to visit Yvonne to see if she was behind the incidents. But they were not that interested. As far as they were concerned, there were real villains to be caught – not lovelorn spinsters.

And when they interviewed Yvonne she really switched on the charm. The two officers came away from her family's farm convinced she was far from a danger to the Smiths. In fact, she seemed like a very nice, responsible sort of person. Hardly the type to carry out a vicious hate campaign. And, even if she was behind some of the incidents, a jilted woman making a pest of herself was hardly an unusual occurance. Let the dust settle and she'll soon give up, the police assured William and Jayne.

Shortly after the wreath incident, Yvonne decided enough was in fact enough – she had to clear her head and try to start afresh.

The first stage in this self-induced rehabilitation was to travel across the nearby border into Scotland, hire a holiday cottage and forget about all her problems. She even got herself a new boyfriend.

In ambulance driver Anthony Berry, she had at last found a new man – whom she felt fond of. At least he satisfied her physically, if not entirely socially. Hidden away in the border country, they could make love until the cows came home. She could put William and all her troubles behind her.

It would be a wonderful break for them both, she told friends. But, inside, the resentment and hatred was still bubbled. She was obsessed with the man who had spurned her. Every time she looked at her lover next to her, she saw William. Every time she walked hand in hand with him through the fields, she saw William.

It was no use pretending. She would have to get him back. Punish that witch Jayne for humiliating her. For making her the laughing stock of all her sneering relatives. For making William turn his back on her when she needed him most.

But, by December 14, Yvonne was like a different person. They had been on holiday for over a week and it was as if all the cares of the world had been lifted from her shoulders. She was beaming with delight. Looking radiant. And best of all she was feeling really passionate.

She had been out for a very long drive alone and now she was back at the cottage, demanding sex from Anthony. Anywhere. She just had to have it – then and there.

He began by probing her mouth deeply with his tongue. Then she allowed him to stroke her body gently. She shut her eyes and savoured the waves of pleasure that coursed through her agile body.

She wanted to imagine it was William, not Anthony, exploring her body. She could see his face, above her, satisfying her, kissing her, loving her. It made the actual sex more enjoyable.

As Yvonne lay there enjoying endless pleasures, she cast her mind back to less than 24 hours earlier. It was a vivid recollection and it made her feel even more aroused.

She had laid patiently in wait for William to leave the farm for his regular game of five-a-side football. After all those years together, how could she forget his soccer. Every Tuesday, without fail, he would go off, leaving his ever-so-sweet little wife all alone at the farm to fend for herself. Alone and vulnerable.

From her vantage point just off the road by the corner, Yvonne knew he would have to pass. She watched silently as his car drove down towards the village. Even though she was not close enough to actually see his face through the car window, she felt a sense of excitement just to know she had been near to him once more.

Soon, she would have him back. He would be hers once more.

She waited patiently in her car. Just in case he returned. He might have forgotten a boot or a sock. She could not be too careful. After ten minutes, she knew he had gone for hours.

She got out of the car and took a deep breath. The wind from the moors whistled furiously around her. The rain was stinging her face as it lashed across the road in front of her. Sometimes the ice cold water would sweep up into a virtual whirlwind before landing with a smack on the tarmac of the road.

It was pitch dark except for the two room lights that shone out from the farm house. The luminous eyes of a fox glanced right in front of Yvonne. The creature scuttled back into the thick undergrowth by the side of the lane. She paused for a moment. Then smiled a knowing sort of smile. A look that said nothing would scare her that night. She glanced up at the farmhouse as a silhouette crossed a window. Sweet little Jayne was in.

As Yvonne walked through the muddy yard towards the front door, she felt a surge of tension go through her body. She was hyped up. Stiff with expectation. She felt that resentment and hatred return once more. It was driving her on all the time. Telling her to continue...

She was breathing quite heavily now. In through her nose, out through her mouth. All the time exercising the muscles of her fingers. Twirling them as if she were about to play the piano. Making sure they were loosened and responsive.

Just two steps from the door, she pushed her hand under her anorak and felt the warm glossy veneer of the wooden handle of the rifle. She pulled it out. It was quite heavy and it took both hands to ease out.

Now she had it pointing downwards with her right

hand on the trigger. Her other hand covered the upper
end of the barrel. She pressed the door bell with the
end of the rifle. It was a cold calculating movement.

Yvonne narrowed her eyes and squinted at the door
as she waited for it to open. The gun now trained dead
centre on the entrance.

Jayne was not the sort of person to worry about
strangers calling at the house at night time. She had
typical country trust – the belief in people's better
natures. She could not imagine anyone wishing her
harm – even after all that fuss with Yvonne.

Jayne had only just got home from her night shift at the
old people's home where she worked as a nurse. There had
not even been time to change out of her uniform.

As she pulled open the door, her pretty face filled with
surprise at first, rather than fear. It was a symptom of that
momentary feeling of disbelief that always occurs when
something completely out of the ordinary happens.

She looked straight at Yvonne. Then at the gun.
Then stood there. Unable to react.

But Yvonne soon broke the silence.

She marched Jayne over to the farmyard. Prodding
her constantly with the gun to keep her moving in the
direction she wanted. Jayne knew precisely what all
this was about.

Yvonne's bitterness had known no limits. Jayne had
over-estimated the woman's better nature.

They stood there, buffetted by the torrential rain.
No conversation between them. Just a rifle barrel for
communication purposes. Pointing right into the back
of Jayne's head. It was the waiting that was the worst.
Waiting for Yvonne to take control and pull the trigger.

She hesitated – not because she was scared. She just
enjoyed the suffering. She wanted to see the pain she
was causing. She felt the urge to flex her fingers once
more. She held the weapon tight in her grasp, remembering everything she had learnt on the rifle range years

before. She didn't want to mess it up. Clean and quick. And oh-so-beautiful.

Yvonne felt the central muscle on her finger squeezing tightly on the trigger. She felt the barrel quiver as the bullet raced into Jayne's head. In a split second it was over.

Yvonne did not panic. She looked at the crumpled body on the muddy yard and realised there was ample time to avoid being accused of this murder. But first, she had to guarantee that he alone would know that she had done it.

She pulled Jayne's limp left hand off the ground and tried to pull off her wedding band. It would not budge. The torrential rain had swollen her finger. Yvonne could do nothing. For a moment, she panicked. The murder had been too easy. But trying to remove her wedding ring was part of her obsession. She had to get it off – no matter what.

She had to know that Jayne would go to her grave without that ring.

She was Mrs William Smith, not Jayne. That scheming bitch had no rights to him in the first place. She had stolen him from her. Now she was denying her the right to remove that ring.

Yvonne would not give up. She struggled to get the ring off. Finally, she managed to twist and turn it enough to pull it up and off her finger.

Elated at her achievement, she now began to consider her next move. People would think it was her. She had to do something to divert attention away from the obvious. That meant making sure it looked like the work of a man.

She crouched down over the body and ripped open the buttoned front of Jayne's nursing tunic. At first, the well-sewn buttons would not give. But, with one almighty yank, they began to pop apart. She stood up and studied her work. It did not look at all convincing. It had to look like the real thing. Not some feeble attempt at pretending it was rape.

Once again, she bent down. All the time the rain was sweeping across her, sometimes hitting her straight in the face. But she knew there was still more work to be done.

She pulled the dress down off her shoulders and arms. Not stopping for a moment to consider the beauty of the person whose life she had just destroyed. She undid the bra and, flexing those fingers like a concert pianist once more, she squeezed the breasts as hard as possible to leave the sort of marks that would be a clear indication of a sexual motive. Men must do that when they rape women, she presumed.

Yvonne was in her element. She loved the organisation side of it. Getting the scene right meant methodical thought, and she had ample supplies of that.

Next, she removed Jayne's pants, nearly slipping in the thick mud as she did so. She pulled them over Jayne's thighs and down the calves towards her slender ankles revealing drenched black stockings.

It was almost over. But not quite. This was supposed to be a sex attack and one vital detail was missing.

She stuffed the sodden pants into her pocket and then lent down, flexing those fingers for the last time...

Yvonne was close to climaxing as Anthony continued heaving himself up and down on top of her.

Her mind had wandered back from the exquisite events of just 20 hours earlier. It seemed like a fantasy. The only reality was that William would soon be hers once more.

After a sensible period of time, she could see the man she really loved again. Then they could marry. Meanwhile Anthony would do. He was a good lover. Anxious to please. Keen to listen.

She felt as though she were in some warm cocoon. Safe in the knowledge that she had committed the killing and she had done everything to put the police off her scent.

The two police officers were charming. They just

wanted to have a few brief words with Yvonne. Anthony let them in immediately.

He was completely unaware of what his lover had done. Yvonne seemed shocked by the news.

"It can't be true. How awful."

Yvonne burst into tears when the officers told her. She was clearly distressed and upset. They had been warned to expect her to be hard nosed and unfeeling about Jayne. But here she was crying profusely. It hardly seemed the reaction of suspected murderess.

The officers said she certainly did not seem to behave like a suspect.

And William's mother could not believe that Yvonne would do such a thing. After all, she received a delightful Christmas card from her the day after Jayne's death.

Inside was a handwritten note. It said: "I have a lovely boyfriend.

"He has been with me for quite some time now... through all the worrying times."

It seemed to convince everyone that she had put all thoughts of ever marrying William firmly out of her mind.

Yvonne posted it just a few hours before she went to Broat's Farm.

She had been very, very meticulous.

William Smith was distraught.

His life was in ruins. He did not know if Yvonne had murdered his wife or not. He was too numb to care about anything except Jayne.

As he hurried along the busy High Street, he knew he had to do one last thing before they buried his darling, beautiful wife.

He frantically looked up and down the road. It was difficult to concentrate in such a bereaved state. But, after a few minutes, he was certain he had found the right shop.

He walked in hesitantly – just in case he was wrong.

But the jeweller recognised him instantly.

"You sold me a ring..."

William started to explain but the man remembered him immediately.

Detective Superintendent Geoff Cash had at last got a breakthrough in the case. Everyone said it must be Yvonne Sleightholme, but the attack seemed to have been carried out by a man with a sexual motive. Then, his officers discovered that she had not been at that cottage in the Scottish borders on the night of the killing.

Then they had found blood stains, matching the victim's group, in Yvonne's car.

Inside the funeral parlour, William Smith walked towards the open coffin – to see his wife for the last time.

She now looked – in death – almost as near to perfection as she had whilst alive.

In a few minutes, they would be taking her away to the funeral ceremony. But for those last few precious moments, he looked at her, remembering all the good times. The wedding. The happy home they shared together. The smiles. The plans.

William lent over the coffin and gently placed the gold ring on Jayne's finger. Now they had become one again. Not even she could take that from them...

On May 10, 1991, Yvonne Sleightholme was jailed for life at Leeds Crown Court.

Shortly after her arrest for the murder of Jayne Smith she was diagnosed as having gone blind following the trauma of the incident.

Judge Mr Justice Waite told Sleightholme: "When your fiancé broke off the engagement and married another woman you wrought upon the newly married couple a terrible revenge.

"You planned in cold fury and executed with ruthless precision the killing of your rival."

10

Victims of the Nazis

The house was simple. Plain bricks. Sloping roof. Nothing too elaborate. It was a bungalow with an abundance of windows but not much character. Set back off the road, its stark, square, modern look made it more in keeping with the suburbs of Los Angeles, than an isolated part of mid-Wales.

It rained a lot in the tiny hamlet of Pant Perthog. The grey clouds and harsh gusts of wind were a permanent feature of life for the handful of residents, yet the climate only helped to emphasize the beauty of the terrain. Lush, rolling hills strewn with acres of ancient woodlands surrounded the village. It was a picture postcard spot where little had changed for over a century.

Just fifty yards to the rear of the bungalow lay the real reason it had been built in the first place. The River Dovey twisted and turned as it snaked a path through the Welsh countryside. Splitting fields in two. Creating bushy river banks amongst little clumps of trees. Providing an excuse for a scattering of those curved, grey stone bridges built so lovingly by the Victorians.

Most properties in the area had their own names like Pear Tree Cottage or Alamo. But the bungalow that Wanda Chantler lived in had no name. Its very existence was enough for her. It was her *home*.

She would have been happy to hide herself away in that house from the world outside. She had no interest in other people. Just eternal gratitude for being alive and well after a life steeped in tragedy.

Wanda and her husband Alan had deliberately chosen the isolated area of Machynlleth as their home because they wanted the peace and solitude that had always eluded them. They really needed the quietness. Both of them had, for too long, been influenced by events that were out of their control. They did not want that any more. They wanted to be in charge of their own destiny.

Wanda had lovingly planned every detail of the construction of the house with her husband Alan 20 years earlier. It became their sanctuary. Their own little piece of paradise in an evil world. An escape from the unspeakable atrocities that occured every day somewhere on the globe. A place where they could bring up their two sons without worry.

And that is what they did. As a family, they became a self-contained unit. Just the four of them. They didn't bother the world and it didn't bother them. They loved to explore the countryside on long rambling walks. Sometimes they would travel to the coast and enjoy a picnic on deserted beaches facing the Atlantic.

But then they made a mistake. A big mistake. After the kids had grown up, they made the heart-wrenching decision to sell the bungalow and head off to Australia to be with one of their sons. It had seemed like the perfect opportunity to come out of their shell-like existance in Pant Perthog and to start to rediscover the outside world. Their plans had failed miserably. Outside of that tiny retreat, they found that nothing had changed.

The same evil forces dominated. The same problems existed. The same wars ravaged on. It was all a bitter disappointment to the Chantlers. They had really hoped and prayed that the new, modern world might be more welcoming. But it was not to be.

Australia wasn't right for them. The idea of sun, sand and sea just did not appeal. The gentle waves of the mid-Wales coastline were a far nicer proposition than the giant surf of Bondi Beach. They felt out of place in an alien world where nearly everyone was under forty.

Wanda, fifty-seven years old, was a highly articulate woman. She always appeared a little dishevelled in a friendly sort of way. She had an intense, introvert manner much of the time. Always slightly on her guard but basically full of good intentions. A trained physiotherapist and a linguist with nine languages to her credit, she found Australia a shallow place. She had little in common with the people she met. She longed to look once more at those lush pastures of Pant Perthog.

Her favourite hobby was painting. She just wanted to have an opportunity to use her water colours to once more re-create that stunning scenery. Back at the bungalow, she used to spend hours lovingly producing her own interpretations of the surrounding countryside. She could lose herself in the paintings. Forget about those painful memories. Only think about the beautiful things in life and put them on canvas.

Alan, just turned 60, felt just as uncomfortable as his wife in the so-called "New World" of Australia. Bespectacled and still with a reasonable head of hair, he was an average looking character. He knew full well how happy Wanda would be to come back to mid-Wales. It meant so much to them both. They were convinced they would feel an immense warmness the moment they arrived once more in the area. They kept wondering why on earth they had sold up their dream to take on a nightmare? It was for the love of the children of course. But they had both grown up by now. They had their own lives to lead. Wanda and Alan needed to get on without them. It would all be so much easier back where they belonged.

So, it was no surprise when Wanda and Alan decided to leave Australia and return to mid-Wales in the late 1970s.

They were so relieved when they arrived back in the area. So delighted to see all those old familiar sights. So enchanted by the slow pace of life. So pleased by the easy going nature of the people. Nothing appeared to have changed.

Everyone welcomed them back to Pant Perthog as

if they had never been away in the first place. That pleasant feeling of warm security began to return as they settled back in the area.

It was so much nicer than Australia. There was a post office and a little shop in the village. Nothing more, nothing less. It was definitely meant to be.

They loved to be able to wander up and down the lanes without that fear of the unknown. The fear they had been haunted by more than 30 years earlier. The fear that returned when they went to live in Australia.

As far as Wanda was concerned, only one thing was still missing. She longed to have that bungalow back. She was desperate to live once again in the place she had been so happy. On the journey back to mid-Wales she kept telling Alan how wonderful it would be to buy the house once again. It held so many cherished memories. He was just as keen, but he feared it might not be as easy as all that.

Wanda's dream really kept her going. She imagined herself back there with all the happy memories of the children.

New owners Roger and Josie Hartland were delighted when they bought the bungalow from the Chantlers. They saw it as their home for the rest of their lives. In much the same way as the Chantlers once had done, they envisaged staying there for ever.

There was something about the area. It was so pure and simple. There were so few complications... until Wanda Chantler returned.

It had been a dream come true for the Hartlands when they bought the place. Roger, 48, had decided he wanted to quit the rat-race and leave his job as an industrial chemist in the Midlands. He couldn't stand the relentless high-pressure existence. Pant Perthog seemed the perfect location and his young wife was just as convinced they were doing the right thing.

They loved the Chantlers' taste. They admired the way they had managed to make a very plain looking house incredibly warm and cosy inside. It had a vital, airy atmosphere. Something that instantly attracted Roger and Josie when they were looking for a home to retire to.

They even felt grateful to the Chantlers for creating such a perfect home and fully appreciated just how heart breaking it had been for them to move out. They tried to reassure them on their move to Australia to join their son.

"It's supposed to be a lovely place. You'll soon settle there."

But the Chantlers' obvious reluctance to move put a sad edge on the whole proceedings. It seemed such a wrench. However, it also showed how much the Chantlers cared – and that was, in a strange sort of way, most reassuring for Roger and Josie. They would have hated to have bought a house from a couple who did not feel any attachment to the place they were leaving. It wouldn't have been the same.

In the end, it was quite a relief when they did actually move in and the Chantlers set off. As they bade farewell to the old couple on their long journey to the other side of the world Roger and Josie presumed that would be the last they would ever see of them.

So when Wanda turned up on their doorstep some three years later, it came as something of a surprise. She still seemed the same gentle, caring creature they had first met. She explained to them how the move to Australia hadn't worked out. The Hartlands felt genuinely sorry for Wanda. She seemed so distressed by it all. They offered her a friendly cup of tea while she poured out all her problems. All the time they were aware that she seemed to want to say something, but kept straying from the point.

They talked about the woods, the river, the trees, the children, the happy memories. But all it did was make Wanda even more sad. Then she changed the whole course of the conversation.

"Would you sell us back the house. We so dearly want it back."

The Hartlands were stunned. They entirely understood her sentiments but they told her firmly how happy they were there and that they could not leave it. They felt awful about the whole situation. They could see from Wanda's response that she really had lived in hope of returning to the place of her dreams.

Most people would have respected the Hartland's decision and left it at that but Wanda would not be that easily deterred. It was the only place where she could put her nightmare to rest. She had to have the bungalow back. It was her only chance to lead a normal life again. If she didn't get it the past would haunt her forever.

All her awful visions were returning. It was as if the occupiers had come back to capture and torture her. The Hartlands were becoming like an army of occupation. They were ordering her not to do something. They wanted to stop her from stepping back inside her mental retreat, preventing her from fleeing the evil forces that had plagued her for more than 40 years.

The shock of their refusal to sell the bungalow threw Wanda back into an awful period of her life. It reopened the wounds that all began in 1939...

She was just 17 years old. Her shoulders were broad but perfectly shaped. Her hair was fair and well-conditioned. Her bone structure was strong and her expression was permanently confident. The picture of an attractive girl on the edge of womanhood.

When her father sent her from their home in Western Russia to law school in Berlin, it seemed a natural step for such an exceptionally talented scholar. The first few months there had been a real eye-opener. Being on her own at such a young age had its problems. She overcame them with her looks. They were her passport to a good time. Berlin was a debauched but exciting place in those days. The sense of danger on the streets was always prevalent, but that made it all the more intriguing if you lived there. There were soldiers on every corner but they didn't bother her except to make fresh remarks about her legs. The bars and cafes of Berlin were wonderful. Packed with artists and writers, oblivious to the repressive regime they lived under.

It was an experience of a lifetime for Wanda. She was learning so much. More than she could ever have hoped for back in Russia. And at the end of her three year stay, she would return home as a trained lawyer. It was an achievement that would really mean something to her family. Maybe she could work abroad? That would be even more fun. The world was at her feet. There was so much she could do with her life, so many possible avenues to go down. She could do whatever she wanted. Nobody and nothing could stop her. Or so she thought...

At first, she did not even notice the street violence involving the soldiers with their Swastika armbands. Her mind was focussed on her ambition to succeed. Everything else took second place.

"Outside now!"

The German soldiers did not waste time with explanations.

They were rounding up every name on a list – and Wanda was one of them. She did not know where she was being taken or why. But the look of fear etched on the others' faces told her enough.

They were all students. Young, highly articulate people. None of it made sense. *They* weren't the enemies of the Germans. They were just studying in Berlin. What was behind all this?

Maybe it was all just a mistake and in a few hours they would be released. But the hours soon turned into days and the days into weeks.

They wanted to know her name, her age, her qualifications. They were particularly interested in her intelligence. They fired question after question at her.

How many languages do you speak? What are your qualifications? What is your father's profession? It went on and on and it was becoming very clear that they had something in mind for Wanda. Something awful was about to happen. It would not have been so bad if she knew what it was. The uncertainty was causing the most pain. She was well aware the time would come when they would take her away to some dreadful place.

She thought of escape. But the opportunity never arose.

Soon Wanda was transferred to a prison unlike any she had ever heard about before. It was more like a farm. There were lots of children. Well, very young adults. Nearly all girls. Everyone was relatively free compared to the previous compound. But that very liberty unnerved her. There was something strange about the place. On the surface it seemed like a school in the country or a holiday camp. Underneath, however, you could taste the misery. Students played on the grass in front of the building, but none of them were smiling. And always in the background were the guards with their stiff uniforms and menacing rifles.

All the girls had a certain attractiveness. They had good figures, exquisite faces – and they all shared the same blank look of fear. None of them seemed to know why they were there.

One younger girl – she must have been about 14 – was crying on the shoulders of another. But Wanda didn't know why. It was an uncertainty which would haunt her for the rest of her life.

The guards were young as well, with many still in their teens. Most of them looked typically German. Well built. Blond hair. Big jackboots. It was the real adults who seemed the most terrifying. There were doctors and nurses everywhere bustling around the place.

One day Wanda was subjected to a physical examination the like of which she had never before experienced in her entire life. She thought it was going to be a straight-forward medical. It turned out to be an horrific encounter. Something she would never forget.

The doctors examined each of the girls in turn with clinical inquisitiveness. Probing every orifice. The pain when one male doctor roughly examined her made Wanda wince. Then they checked her general health, her strength and fitness. Still Wanda was bemused. Why were all these doctors examining her? What were they planning? She was blissfully unaware that anyone who failed those first medicals went straight to the death camps.

They lived in ignorance for weeks. They were well fed, given many books to read, encouraged to learn and subjected to numerous tests.

Wanda soon realised the doctors were pleased with her. They would say words like "perfect" and "beautifully formed" as though they were describing animals rather than human beings.

Then one morning, Wanda was ordered to see the camp's chief physician. She wondered what it was about. She had passed the tests. What more could they possibly want to do to her?

When she walked into the room, there, standing with the doctor, was a tall, well-built German with blond hair and chiselled features like a cardboard cutout

He examined Wanda with his sharp crystalline eyes. Looking up and down her body as she stood there. At first, they said nothing. She was just ordered to stay still and not speak – just allow this total stranger to cast his eyes all over her body.

The doctor turned to the man and said, "What do you think."

That word "perfect" was used yet again.

It was at last starting to dawn on Wanda why she was there. The doctors. The man. The questions. She was terrified. All the nightmare scenarios she had considered were now coming true.

She had been nurtured and fed at that farm in order to create the perfect baby for the perfect race. She was to become a surrogate mother for the Aryan race – Hitler's consuming obsession.

She was a virgin faced with conveyor belt sex on demand. No emotion. No love.

Wanda was taken into an adjoining room. In the corner was a mattress. She was forced to strip off her clothes...

Forty years later in Pant Perthog, Wanda was reliving that dreadful nightmare. She couldn't get the sex farm out of her mind. Of course, she had thought about it every day for the whole of her life. No one could forget what had happened. But before, she had control over those feelings. Now, she was consumed with out and out anger. The Hartland's were standing in her way. Punishing her. Hadn't she already had punishment enough? She couldn't allow it. She had to do something.

They had become Nazi guards. Their refusal to sell the house was as much an atrocity to her as the behaviour of those blond Aryan brutes.

Wanda's husband Alan was beside himself with worry. He could see his wife's obsession growing at an alarming rate. He tried to explain that there were other places to live. But nowhere except the bungalow would do for Wanda.

The Hartland's would have to suffer for the torture they had inflicted on her.

Wanda's first step was to enroll at the local gun club.

The Aberyswyth Rifle Club was the sort of place that is frequented mainly by men. Set in the heart of the Welsh countryside, it was primarily used by genuine enthusists and responsible farmers trying to keep in their aim.

When Wanda first showed up to learn skills with a gun, there were a few raised eyebrows, but the members soon became used to seeing the grandmotherly figure cocking a weapon to her shoulder and firing off round after round of bullets.

She rapidly gained a reputation as a very fine shot. No-one asked her why she wanted to learn in the first place. They aren't like that in mid-Wales. Mind your own business, ask no questions and life will stay easy.

Her aim became deadlier by the day

Josie Hartland was close to tears as she screwed up the letter that had just come through the post box of their house. She was worried by the threats. What made it worse was the fact they both knew exactly who had written it. Wanda Chantler.

It was the third letter to have arrived in a couple of weeks. Each one had become more elaborate. More sinister. And now it mentioned treasure hidden under the bath.

Wanda Chantler was becoming increasingly withdrawn. She and her husband had found a place to live at nearby Garth Owen. But it wasn't the same as the bungalow. The countryside didn't look or sound the same. It was more built up. More noisy. Less private.

Living there made Wanda even more obsessed with moving back to the bungalow. She hated meeting people in the street near their new home. They just didn't seem so friendly.

Wanda felt less and less inclined to go out. Apart from her trips to the rifle club she rarely left the house. Alan Chantler was becoming increasingly worried about his wife's health and mental state. All she could talk about was the bungalow. How she had to have it back. He kept telling her to forget it. But she would have none of it.

She started to convince herself that she had left some hidden treasure under the bath. A lot of gold trickets and an assortment of other things. Losing the house was bad enough, but the treasure was legally hers. She was the rightful owner. No-one should be allowed to take that away from her. She kept asking the Hartlands, and they said it did not exist. But she knew it was there. She knew it.

Wanda began to write another letter. This time it was to the local paper. The venom soon flowed. Her targets were the Hartlands. If she could not persuade them to give up her house – the house she created and made into what it was today – then she would hound them until they hated the very sight of it.

"You have got to do something. The woman is deranged."

Roger Hartland had had enough of the threats. His wife was in tears when he had got home that day. It was an outrage that anyone could make such vicious comments about someone they hardly knew.

Something had to be done, so he turned to the police.

Crime was almost non-existent in Pant Perthog. Nothing much ever happened. And that made it all the more difficult for the police to respond rapidly to any problem that might arise. The officers were sympathetic. But how could anyone take a grandmother's threats seriously? There was no possiblity of her carrying them out.

Roger Hartland was convinced otherwise. He believed that Wanda Chantler's threats had the ring of authenticity about them. That was why they were so frightening.

"Just give us a call if you have any more problems."

The policeman was merely doing his duty, but no more. This sort of thing never happened in a place like Pant Perthog, after all. Why should it start now?

Alan Chantler also knew otherwise. He was well aware of Wanda's obsessive nature, after nearly 40 years of marriage. After all, they had first met when he and his fellow allied troops arrived at the sex farm in 1945 and liberated the inhabitants. It was an emotionally draining job. But it had one reward – he met Wanda.

Within a short time, they had married and moved to Britain. Those past horrors seemed to have been put behind them. Wanda never really spoke much about the farm. She bottled it all up. Thinking constantly about it but never telling her closest friend. It had to come out sooner or later.

Alan was well aware his wife was on the verge of a nervous breakdown. She had become agrophobic – refusing to leave their new home for anything other than rifle club training.

Reluctantly, he went to the police and got her shotgun licence revoked before any tragedy could occur. Instinctively, he knew she was heading in that direction. He could feel each second ticking away before his wife's inevitable explosion. He was convinced it was only a matter of time before something awful happened. The threats, the letters. She had even been around to the Hartlands to try to frighten them into selling the house.

Wanda's main topic of conversation at home was the treasure under the bath. Alan knew it didn't exist but he also knew that in his wife's mind it was the only piece of reality she could still cling to.

The Hartlands were as bad as the SS in her eyes. Maybe they even came from Germany, she thought.

In Wanda's mind, the sex farm and the Hartlands were rapidly becoming synonymous with each other. Maybe they took their orders from the camp commandant? Perhaps they had been sent here to hunt her down and take her back?

One sunny Monday, June 16, 1980, Wanda Chantler plunged into the abyss of insanity.

At Garth Owen, Wanda was in a better mood than she had been for weeks. Alan was delighted by this improvement in his wife's health and decided to leave her for a few hours to do the shopping.

The moment he left the house, she scurried to the wardrobe to get dressed. She felt good inside herself. There was a job to be done. She had an objective for the first time in months. It gave her a fresh appetite for life. Maybe that had been the problem all along? She needed to have something to achieve. Life had to have its goals otherwise what was the point in existing?

205

Josie Chantler was feeling in the same sort of mood over at Pant Perthog. She was getting on with the household chores like washing and cleaning the kitchen and all the other essential work of the day. She enjoyed keeping the bungalow clean and fresh.

The weather made her feel happy as well. It was so rare to get a really nice day in these parts.

The last few weeks had been blissfully clear of problems from *that* woman. It seemed they had heard the last of her.

Wanda pulled her car up about fifty yards from the entrance to the bungalow, just out of sight of the actual property. She opened the boot, took out two air pistols and tucked them over each hip cowboy fashion.

Then she lifted out the double barrelled shotgun. It was much heavier than the pistols. But then it was also far more lethal.

Lastly, she took out that treasured painting of the landscape surrounding the bungalow – one of the pictures she had toiled over so lovingly all those years before.

She looked an incongruous sight with the thick leather belt strapped around her waist over a very tweedy, country outfit. If it were not for the guns, she would have looked like a typical country squire's wife out for a walk in the country.

It was quite difficult to carry the shotgun and the painting. But Wanda managed. The determination was there. She could achieve anything that day.

She had to get away from the Nazis. Get them out of her life for ever. Destroy them before they destroyed her.

As she walked up to the front door, her mind kept flashing back to the sex farm. The experiments, the examinations, the clinical rape. This time she would rid herself of those memories once and for all.

She would have her revenge. *And* her treasure under the bath. *And* her bungalow.

206

She thought she was back in Germany. It all seemed so clear.

"I have a present for you."

The Hartlands were stunned when they opened the front door to see Wanda standing, armed like some sort of elderly, female Rambo, on the step.

"It's a painting I did of the area. I thought you would like it."

"You've got to come quickly. She's got three guns..."

The Hartlands' telephone call to Alan Chantler was still remarkably calm, considering the arsenal of weapons she had on her.

She waited on the doorstep.

Roger Hartland went to open the front door to tell her that Mr Chantler was on his way. Wanda aimed the shotgun straight at the entrance. As it opened, Roger saw the barrel pointing right at him for a split second before it went off.

The sheer force of the shot sent him to the ground in a crumpled heap.

Inside, Josie Hartland was grappling for the phone. Dialing 999. She just hoped the operator would answer quickly. She got through, but was told to wait for a police officer to come on the line. Seconds passed while she waited for the answer. Still there was no-one at the other end of the line. When would they come? Hurry. Hurry. Hurry.

Wanda was now in the bungalow, seeking out her tormentors. She entered the kitchen quietly to see Josie cowering in a corner of the room with the phone, frantically shouting down the receiver in the desperate hope someone would help her.

But all she had in fact done was lead Wanda to her. Wanda stood for a moment and stared at Josie before cocking her gun.

The two shots hit her full on. But she was still alive. Still struggling for breath.

Wanda calmly reloaded the shotgun and fired another shot. One was enough to finish off the enemy. They were so weak when you confronted them. Cowards squirming pathetically in a corner. She hadn't even used up all her rounds.

On 24 October, 1980, Wanda Chantler admitted the manslaughter of the Hartlands and was sent to Broadmoor Hospital without limit of time.

Sentencing her, Mr Justice Hodgson, said: "Nobody could possibly have heard what we have here without feeling the most terrible compassion. In a sense, you are as much a victim of your Nazi experiences as the Hartlands were victims of that same horror."